The Duchess Contest

A Jet City Billionaire Romance

Gina Robinson

THREE JAYS PRESS, LLC
SEATTLE, WASHINGTON

www.ginarobinson.com

Publisher's Note: This is a work of fiction. Names, characters, places, and incidents are a product of the author's imagination. Locales and public names are sometimes used for atmospheric purposes. Any resemblance to actual people, living or dead, or to businesses, companies, events, institutions, or locales is completely coincidental.

Book Layout ©2013 BookDesignTemplates.com
Cover Design by Jeff Robinson

The Duchess Contest, The Billionaire Duke Series/Gina Robinson.
— 1st ed.
ISBN 978-0692636282

Also by
GINA ROBINSON

THE BILLIONAIRE DUKE SERIES
Part 1, THE BILLIONAIRE DUKE
Part 2, THE DUCHESS CONTEST

SWITCHED AT MARRIAGE ROMANCE
SERIAL
Part 1, A WEDDING TO REMEMBER
Part 2, THE VIRGIN BILLIONAIRE
Part 3, TO HAVE AND TO HOLD
Part 4, FROM THIS DAY FORWARD
Part 5, FOR RICHER, FOR RICHEST
Part 6, IN SICKNESS AND IN WEALTH
Part 7, TO LOVE AND TO CHERISH

NEW ADULT ROMANCE
RUSHED
CRUSHED
HUSHED
RECKLESS LONGING
RECKLESS SECRETS
RECKLESS TOGETHER

SPY CAMP BOOKS
SPY CANDY
SPY GAMES

THE AGENT EX SERIES

CHAPTER ONE

*S*eattle, Washington
Riggins, reluctant Duke of Witham
The media—American and British—was in a complete frenzy over my status as an American duke and running high with speculation. What had started as a small, inconsequential human-interest spark had grown into epic forest fire of headline-grabbing proportions. The stories fed on themselves and gobbled up the time and attention of social media and the entertainment shows the way flames consume oxygen. Every time I got online, another hashtag about me was trending.

#DuchessSearch #AmericanOrBritish
#LetMeBeTheOne
#ShutUp #LeaveMeTheHellAlone

The last two were mine. And existed only in my head. I wasn't dumb enough to post them. I didn't respond at all. My accounts were overwhelmed with friend requests. I ignored them and turned off all notifications.

The British press had been working overtime while I slept, fitfully, after dropping Haley off after our ball for two, just me and her. My mind raced with thoughts of her. The scent of her perfume. The way she laughed. The sparkle in her two mismatched eyes. Whatever Milia had done to her, she'd done too damn well. Though, deep down, I had to admit, it wasn't all Milia's handiwork. Haley had a natural charm all her own that was hard to resist.

But if I was throwing blame around, I had to take my share. It was my own fault for asking Milia to make Haley into duchess material. I should have known Milia would be unable to resist the temptation to make her into a femme fatale. Milia was vindictive that way. Determined to change the course of my life that she believed she'd altered. It was egotistical of her to hold that opinion. But neither of us were known for our humility. That had been part of our problem.

She thought I needed love in my life. She was atoning for breaking my heart. She took too much credit for my single status. She didn't realize I'd chosen this life. It was what I wanted and suited me just fine. *Shit.* I needed my head about me, not the distraction of a love affair.

Haley had done something no woman had done to me in years—intrigued me. Shown me a glimpse of something pure and genuine. Something I'd forgotten existed. Or maybe something I'd thought had died. Shown me what regular life was like. Despite all the hoopla surrounding us, when it was just her and me, I was a regular guy. She made me remember what it had been like when I'd been unknown Riggins, a broke college kid. Leading a regular life out of the spotlight. Back when I'd known that a woman was with me because she liked *me*. Not my money.

Funny to think those thoughts about Haley being with me for me when Thorne had coerced Haley into dating me. But, hell, she wasn't with me for my money. Not in the usual way. Not using me. If anything, we were protecting each other. It had been a long time since I'd had a woman on my side. It felt too damn good.

If I could have picked my ally, I would have chosen someone like Milia—strong, smart, savvy, competent beyond belief. However, Haley was refreshingly naïve. Soft. Sweet. Unjaded. Funny. Witty. Alluring. *Genuine. Honest.* There was something to be said for all that.

I couldn't get her out of my head. Though I was damn well going to try. For now, we were allied by our common interest in surviving and foiling the Dead Duke's plans. But what did we really have in common?

No. I was better off alone. I wasn't ready to give up my freedom. Or share my life and private time. Especially not if I was forced into it.

On Sunday morning, after my date with Haley, I was in my home office early. Working with a cup of coffee at my side. Trying to find a way out of this marriage mess and defeat the wily Dead Duke. If I was going to outwit him, I had to think like him. Know your enemy.

Because he was dead, I couldn't sit down with him face to face and feel him out. See how he thought. I was reduced to playing biographer and historian and re-searching everything I could about him online. Where there was precious little about such a long-lived duke.

I hated to admit it to myself, but the best place to study him was Witham House, where I would have ac-cess to everything he'd left behind. Diaries. Personal papers. Personal effects. Paintings of our ancestors hanging on the walls. There *had* to be some clue to him and the way he thought there.

I would have been on a plane for Heathrow in a se-cond, if I didn't suspect I would be playing right into his hands. If I were the Dead Duke, I would try to lure me to the estate. Where he could play the game several ways. One, hope I would fall in love with the place and develop an attachment to it. Make it so pleasant and perfect I would never leave.

Or, two, burden me with emergency after urgent matter, keeping me there indefinitely and diverting me from my real mission of trying to get out of marrying. Old-time heirs who didn't want to marry put it off as long as possible. And did crazy crap to try to get out of it. I was no different. Only this pressure was something else.

Or, three, the Dead Duke would use some legal mat-ter to keep me in England.

As tempting as it was to go to Witham House, I had my reservations. I had a gut feeling it wouldn't be good. I decided to stay put in Seattle for now and take care of business. Flash needed my attention. I damn well wasn't going to let this duke distraction take my eye off the ball and ruin Flash all by myself.

At six thirty, my phone rang, jarring me out of the thoughts I'd been lost in. I got a desperate call from my personal assistant Jennifer.

"Riggins! Thank God. How can you be so calm? My phone hasn't stopped ringing since five this morning. I would have turned it off and let those media dogs howl, but the speculation is getting ridiculous. If it keeps up, you're going to have to put our PR department on it to do damage control. And hire an answering service and talent agent."

"Talent agent?" I took a sip of coffee and frowned.

"Oh, yeah. A big-time one. I'm being bombarded with calls from journalists and from producers and their assistants begging me to set up interviews with you. Asking personal questions about you.

"I swear every reality dating show producer on the planet—from both American and British versions—has been in touch with offers. Some have even proposed developing a new show just for you—*The Bachelor Duke*. A wonderful show about a duke, you, who must find a duchess and is offered at least twenty gorgeous, carefully screened candidates. Women who can offer great, entertaining television, as well as have the qualifications to be wonderful duchesses.

"There will be the bitch, naturally. You won't choose her. And the long shot. The small-town girl from next door. You know, your basic Cinderella kind. In a mere twenty weeks, or less, of show time, you'll have a bride. The show will end with you proposing to one lucky lady. And in this case, she may be a real lady.

"The producer even offered to make it a combined American/British version, evenly populated with duchess hopefuls from both countries. And lessons for the American girls on how a duchess should behave. With lessons for the British girls on American, specifically Seattle, culture and how to be the wife of an American billionaire. Sound good, Your Grace?" She sounded tired and harried, but her tone was light and teasing.

"No," I said.

"No?" Jennifer said. "That's it? No explanation? I could say it's beneath the dignity of a duke."

"That's it. Just no. No show. No interviews."

"All right. You're the boss, but this isn't going away."

"Who the hell came up with these ideas?" I was getting suspicious. I wondered if something had leaked. "Why does everyone think I want to get married immediately?"

Jennifer laughed again. "Have you been in isolation? Clearly you haven't seen the online news and blogs. They're claiming that they have exclusive information from a source, who spoke on condition of anonymity that, as the last living Feldhem, you're concerned about dying without an heir. So you're looking to marry and produce one as soon as possible."

Jennifer laughed at that. Like it was absurd. "They're painting a fairytale, romantic view of your situation. Saying you're looking for your soulmate and will stop at nothing to find her."

I rolled my eyes. "That's so much bullshit."

"It's what they're claiming. Which brings me to my next point—the matchmakers and online dating services that have been offering their services. Several of the major online dating sites would love to offer you the job as their spokesman, complete with endorsement bonuses. Including complimentary matchmaking services."

I cursed beneath my breath.

Jennifer kept talking. "Several private, exclusive matchmakers have been in touch, too. They're more discreet. And they want to be *paid* for their services. But they will carefully screen candidates.

"They guarantee their potential duchesses will all have the right pedigree, background checks that include their financial status and criminal record—no murderesses, I presume—and be screened for complete compatibility with you. Using their scientific methods for creating matches. Some of these services have impressive credentials."

"I bet they do."

"For an additional fee—I'm not kidding here—they will also screen them to be sure they're fertile and capable of producing the heir you so desire. And get them to sign a legal document giving you full custody of an heir in the case of divorce."

"*What?*"

"I know!" She sighed. "You can't make this stuff up."

I looked out over Lake Washington and scowled. *Thorne.* He had to be behind this leak. *Anonymous source. Right.* This was his attempt to force my hand. Into marriage.

"The answer is still no. I can find my own bride. Why would I need their help?"

Jennifer laughed. "Got it."

"What else are they saying? Anything?"

"You have a British fan club now."

"What?" Just what I needed. "Why the hell do I have a fan club?"

Jennifer laughed. "You should really Google yourself once in a while. The British press is advocating for a British duchess. A group of women have gotten together and formed a fan club. It's really more of a group of duchess hopefuls. Their club goal is to find you a British duchess. They're chartering a plane over in the hopes of meeting you. They've been in contact, asking for a meeting with you."

"No. Hell no."

"You're becoming fond of that word, boss. Don't dismiss your fan club out of hand. The new president is fairly attractive."

I sighed. "Keep this up and—"

"I'll demand hazard pay. I can't leave my house. There's a horde of reporters out front and it's not even light out yet."

"You should have mentioned that first. Call our security team and tell them to take care of it. Bill it to me—"

A helicopter flew over the house, cutting off her response.

"Sorry. Couldn't hear you," I said. As the helicopter circled back, I caught a silhouette of a guy with a camera in the passenger seat. Damn, a film crew.

"Will do," she repeated. "Was that a helicopter I heard?"

I sighed. "The media circus has reached me here at home." I shook my head. "I'm sorry about the inconvenience, Jennifer."

"Don't apologize. It's adding a little excitement to my life. As long as it doesn't last forever, I'm good."

The exact terms of the will, and whom I must marry, had evidently remained under wraps. Giving girls the world over false hope of winning my heart. *Shit.* A fan club? Things were worse than I thought.

Any woman *might* win my heart. *Good luck with that.* But winning the role of my duchess fell to one particular set of DNA.

After I hung up with Jennifer, I got online and read the latest buzz on me. I laughed at the unwitting British entertainment media advocating heavily for a British duchess. It was a travesty, an insult against the British citizenry, that the first eligible duke to come on the market in years was, for all intents and purposes, an American. The gossip magazines and entertainment shows were full of speculation.

It was bad enough, after all, to have a duke with definite American heritage and leanings. I was an anomaly. A curiosity. A fantasy. And an eligible duke in a market sadly lacking in dukes with estates intact.

If I'd been a character in one of my mom's old Regency romances, or Jane Austen's era, I would have been forced to attend balls at Almack's and faced the marriage mart as dozens of eligible girls were paraded before me. It appeared that times hadn't changed much in essentials. The marriage mart had moved online and become high tech.

The helicopter departed, flying off toward the south and Renton Field. As the sun came up, a movement outside my window caught my attention.

What the hell?

A drone flew up to my window.

I had had enough. I grabbed a remote control out of my desk drawer and called my self-defense drone. My enemy-drone-netting drone. A minute later, my drone successfully brought down the enemy drone. All that video game playing finally came in handy for something. I called security to come get the captured drone and asked them to put a special drone-detecting detail on. Any more drones invaded my personal airspace, my team was under orders to take them out. This was getting ridiculous.

My phone buzzed again. Thorne calling. What did he want?

I picked up. "If it isn't the emissary of Satan calling. Hello, Thorne."

"Nice speaking to you, too, Your Grace."

He was imperturbable.

"To what do I owe the pleasure?" I leaned back in my chair and watched one of my security guys cart off the enemy drone. Which, in all likelihood, belonged to some overzealous member of the paparazzi.

"You may have heard. A British woman has come forward claiming to be a descendant of the late duchess."

"What?" My face lit up. I couldn't help it. If this news upset Thorne, it had to be good for me.

"Yes, I apologize, Your Grace. Her name is Rosanagh Lily Browne. She goes by Rose. *Lady* Rose. Her father is the Earl of Colchester. Which makes the matter more delicate. I very much doubt she's discovered the full terms of the late duke's will—"

"Don't look at me," I said. "I sure as hell wouldn't tell anyone."

"I wasn't making any accusations, sir." Thorne rustled some papers on his end. "The news of an American woman inheriting a small token from the estate has been all over British media. Lady Rose claims she saw the news story on Miss Hamilton and couldn't believe her good fortune in finding another blood relation so soon. Previously, she didn't know any existed."

"You missed a descendant?" I said, both amused and disturbed. Almost excited. Thorne and the Dead Duke were fallible. Which gave me hope that they'd tripped up on something essential. That I could still foil them.

At the same time, this wasn't shaping up to be any better news for me. Except potentially I now had a whopping choice of two women to be my bride. Unless she was already married. Or not of childbearing age.

"We were very thorough. We didn't miss anyone, I assure you." Thorne sounded indignant. "She's *claiming* she was given up for adoption at birth. But that she is a biological descendant of the late Helen Feldhem, Duchess of Witham.

"She's a socialite and minor celebrity in the UK. She was on a British TV show recently that traced her roots back to Helen. The episode is set to air in a few weeks."

"But does she have proof?" I asked.

"I've not spoken with her directly. She claims the show has authenticated the paper trail that traces her ancestry. On the surface, it appears her claims are accurate, that she is descended from the late duchess. I need to look into the matter further. I've already set my people on it. My private investigator's team is hard at work now, trying not to draw any attention to our interest in her.

"If her claim is proven, the terms of the late duke's will include her. You could have a choice of two women for your bride. Which will make the late duke extremely unhappy. He hand-selected Miss Hamilton for you."

I took that in, holding in a laugh at the Dead Duke's potential unhappiness. How could a dead guy be anything? Unless he was coming back to haunt me, I didn't give a damn. "A choice of two women. That's good news. I'm all for choices." I couldn't help teasing Thorne. I still had no intention of marrying anyone.

"I wouldn't trust her, sir," Thorne said. "There are rumors her father is in desperate financial straits. On the verge of losing what's left of his ancestral home. He funds Lady Rose's lifestyle. If he loses it all, so does she. She isn't the kind of young woman to take to econo-mizing kindly.

"It's my guess she smells money. I wouldn't be sur-prised if she decides to contest the will. Greed, Your Grace, drives many ambitions.

"At this point, she doesn't know the details of the will, including the marriage clause. I can stall while I verify her claim. If she is who she says she is, I will be obligated to share the terms of the will with her.

"Whether she would be willing to step into the role of your duchess isn't certain. However, to a certain type of person, money of this kind would tempt them to do anything." He sounded disgusted and offended. Disap-proving of this new descendant on principle.

I laughed. "Is this new chick hot?"

"Sorry, Your Grace?"

"Is she attractive? You're supposed to be screening for these things."

"I couldn't say for certain. I haven't met her in per-son. If her pictures are an accurate representation, she looks fashionable and put together."

"Don't be so cagey, Thorne. I want all the details."

I imagined Thorne trying to suppress a sigh. "She *claims* to be single."

"Claims?"

"In cases like this, it's always best to make sure. Con artists out for money make all kinds of promises and claims. It's best not to get embroiled in a scandal like Lady Ellen, who married a married man and left her fortune and estate in legal turmoil and her family name in tatters. Of course, she didn't know he was married. He claimed he was divorced. But there you have it. The two of them were conning Lady Ellen.

"We need to make sure Lady Rose isn't mistaken about her biological family. And proceed from there."

"How old is she?"

"Twenty-nine. I'll text you her picture. Or search online on your own. You can decide for yourself whether she's attractive or not." He paused. "I want to let you know that I will handle this situation. I very much doubt she is a legitimate descendant."

"Are you making a pun, Thorne?" I laughed.

"Hardly, Your Grace." Thorne paused.

"Won't a simple DNA test verify her claims?" I asked.

"They would, sir. If any of the late duchess' DNA was available to test against. But there isn't any unless we exhume her body. Which would only be a last resort. We only have Miss Hamilton's DNA to test against—the late duke authenticated her line. And we can't compel her to give it to us."

Thorne paused. "It's my opinion that Lady Rose is what you Americans would call a gold digger. Giving her the benefit of the doubt, she is mistaken about her parentage.

"The late duke foresaw situations of this kind arising. His will leaves all of the woman's half of his mother's money to the woman, of the correct bloodline, of course, who *marries* you. And that is the catch. Only your future wife will inherit anything.

"It's my guess that many more of these women will surface the longer you remain single. You already have a fan club, I see."

"So I hear. Word gets around," I said. "What am I supposed to do with them? How do I put a stop to this?"

"Marry Miss Hamilton, and marry her soon."

"But what about poor Lady Rose? Now that I have a choice, shouldn't I explore it? If she and I hit it off, I promise I'll marry *her* ASAP."

"I'm sorry, Your Grace. That would be ill-advised of you. Lady Rose hasn't been vetted. Even if she turns out to be a descendant of the late duchess, she wasn't the late duke's choice.

"Believe me when I say he gave the selection of the next mistress of Witham very much thought and thoroughly vetted Miss Hamilton. She's called out by name in the will. And you do understand that if Lady Rose's claim is allowed to proceed, the details of the will will be made public. At the very least, much more likely to be leaked. Is that really what you want?"

CHAPTER TWO

Haley, the possible future Duchess of Witham

At two a.m., Steve, the weekend manager at the bakery, called and asked me to come in on my day off and pull an extra shift. Someone had called in sick. Working on my days off was becoming a habit. My constant desperate need for money made me willing to come in at a moment's notice and put me on the top of the bakery's call list.

I was awake, anyway, lying in bed, trying to come off the high and fight off panic. That feeling of something beautiful slipping away, or being pulled from my weak grasp. From the fullness of balancing on the precipice of falling in love to the darkness of a dream dying before its time.

My mind was racing, too active to rest. How was it possible to sleep after a date like this? It had been...a fantasy. And yes, I had initially thought the success of the date and the way I was beginning to feel about Riggins meant I would never marry him. But the appearance of this new challenger changed everything.

Riggins' kiss was still light on my lips. I wrapped my arms around myself, remembering the feel of his arms around me. The news from Sid kept interfering with my daydreams, coming between my imaginary Riggins and me.

This Rose, *Lady* Rose, adopted daughter of an earl, appearing out of nowhere. She had to be stopped. *I* had to stop her. For Sid. And, yes, for me. And possibly even for Riggins. My motives for marrying him were pure, at least. What would hers be? Social climbing?

I kept telling myself, *He doesn't want to marry you.*

The point could be made that he didn't want to marry *anyone.* And that I wasn't ready to get married, either. Certainly not after knowing him less than a week. That this might be nothing more than one of those crushes that burns quickly and dies out. By this time next week the infatuation, love, whatever it was, could die. And I would find myself noticing his every flaw and wondering what, exactly, had made him so attractive.

Realistically, though? I couldn't see that happening. Not with a guy like Riggins. Although I had a habit of falling hard and fast for guys, and regretting it quickly afterward, this felt different. And not just because of the circumstances. This felt...*real.*

After such a fantastic date, I would have had a hard time sleeping, anyway. But now there was *her*. The eleventh-hour competition. I felt my dreams of never having to answer a work call in the dead of night again slipping away.

I didn't like to admit it, but deep down, I think I had felt secure in my power. Smug. I was the last of my line. The last single female of childbearing age in the late duchess' family. Unless Riggins could find a way to break the Dead Duke's hold on us, we were "stuck" with each other and no one else. And even if he *did* find a way, it meant a cure for Sid and plenty of money for me, anyway.

That old line about not realizing what you have until it was gone made scary sense to me now. I couldn't believe I had been considering *not* marrying him. I'd been so dumb and innocent, thinking everyone was good and kind. That no one would try to take him away from me while he played knight valiant and fought for our freedom. That greed didn't exist in our world.

I'd had the duchess fantasy for less than a week and already some British bitch was trying to take it away. Where had she come from? How real were her claims? How could Thorne have missed her? He'd seemed so...so...so *competent*.

Assuming her claim was legitimate, with Rosanagh Lily Browne—first name pronounced like the American name Rosanna. (Yes, I looked it up. Silly English names. You'd think they spoke a whole different language.) Anyway, with Lady Rose, in the picture, Riggins had an alternative to buying me off. He could marry *her* instead. What if a dozen more English Roses popped up? Or a hundred? Riggins couldn't buy them *all* off. Sooner or later, the safest thing for him to do was marry. Me. Or one of them.

I felt sick at the thought. I felt Sid's cure slipping through my fingers and my happiness fading away.

I cursed my trusting nature. I needed a lawyer. A *good* one. Someone schooled in unconventional law and relationships. If only I'd already had one draw up an agreement between Riggins and me, I wouldn't be in this mess. Riggins would be bound to honor a signed document, a contract. I'd waited too long. Just days had been too long. I didn't even know *how* to find a good lawyer. Or have the money to pay for one. All that talk in Thorne's office had just been bravado. When it came down to actually acting on it, I was at a loss.

I needed to talk to Thorne. I sent him a frantic text to call me as soon as possible. What was he doing about this new woman? Did he know about her? Was he playing us, too? Was this part of the Dead Duke's strategy to get Riggins to marry and reproduce? Did she have a legal right to be the next duchess?

I Googled Lady Rose. Read everything about her that I could find. Facebook-stalked her. Stalked all of her social media accounts. What I read and saw made me more and more anxious.

She was evidently a popular British socialite. A social media hound who'd been romantically linked over the years to some of Britain's hottest bachelors. The kind of woman who cultivated fame and media attention for sport. She had over a hundred thousand Twitter followers! One hundred thousand. The number boggled my mind. She tweeted everything, little miss social media butterfly. Including how excited she was about meeting her only living biological relative. Funny she didn't want to meet Sid. Adopted relatives apparently didn't count. Kind of ironic, considering.

And now she was invading the American press, courting the American entertainment shows, trending on social media in America. She was sly and well-schooled in getting attention, I would give her that.

Lady Rose was even listed in Britain's ultimate guide to the peerage. Yes, fascinating reading. I found that online, too.

She was the adopted daughter of the Earl of Colchester and his second wife. His second *ex*-wife of four. The earl apparently believed in marriage, but had a roving eye his wives found hard to ignore. He had several biological children with each of his various other wives. But Lady Rose was the only adopted one.

Her parents divorced when she was four. She'd been raised by her social-climbing mother, who'd never managed to snag another title above countess again. Lady Rose had gone to a prestigious British public school. Which was confusing. Here in the States we'd call it a private school.

She was a British socialite who apparently was determined to emulate certain American women who'd become famous for being famous. She'd recently found her biological roots after being a minor celebrity guest on a BBC program that traced celebrities' ancestors for them. The episode was scheduled to air soon. But Lady

Rose had let the cat out of the bag early. The show had managed to crack the seal of her adoption records and trace her family tree back to Seattle and early twentieth-century heiress Helen Wares, later the Duchess of Witham.

Helen's father William Wares had been a lumber baron, made a killing in the rebuilding of Seattle after the great fire of 1889 destroyed the city. And selling to the railroads. All those railroad ties had to come from somewhere. His name was still big in lumber circles, apparently. Though the company he founded had gone public long ago and eventually gotten into paper production and, more recently, technology.

Wasn't that good luck for Lady Rose, finding me now at the height of her quest for fame?

It hadn't taken her long to sniff out the story and insert herself in it. And on paper, at least, she looked eminently more qualified for the role of duchess than I was. Did she know she was one of only two contenders for the title?

I rode the bus to work, nervously killing time, waiting for Mr. Thorne to call or text me back. He was staying in Seattle until Riggins and I settled things, i.e. married. He'd been right not to trust us. But if he'd been in London, he would have been up and available.

Lady Rose had only come on the scene yesterday, and already she was almost more of a celebrity than Riggins as she flitted from interview to interview. Gushing about how excited she was at the thought of meeting another biological relative—me.

She'd thought she was the last. She was thrilled to find out she had an American relative. She would just *love* to meet me. And, of course, the new duke. Because, in a way, they were related too! They both shared in the heritage of Witham House! How lovely.

Right. I bet she *would* like to meet Riggins. Was she the kind of woman who would be happy to marry for money and a title? Thrilled, even. Maybe it was the goal of her life. Looking at her previous dating history, I guessed it was.

And what was all this about a fan club? Riggins had a fan club. A plane full of his groupies was scheduled to arrive on Monday. It would have been funny, hysterical even, if it had been happening to *someone else.* The whole situation was ridiculous.

So now I had this Rose person to contend with *and* a flight of fancy to fend off. Seriously, what was next?

I had Sid to think about. If someone else caught Riggins' eye, who knew what he would do? I'd been so waffly. So congenial. So willing to go along with Riggins' plan that I'd screwed up and maybe screwed Sid and me out of the money we needed. And me out of something wonderful with Riggins.

I usually loved the city early in the morning when it was almost quiet, the way it was when I showed up for work. But I barely noticed it. I arrived in my baker's whites, hair pulled up and in a hairnet, bags beneath my eyes.

On Saturday mornings there were usually two bakers on staff. Cody was the other one working. *Great.*

"If it isn't the duchess. I didn't expect *you* to show up today after a night out with a billionaire. Shouldn't you be calling in rich?"

Duchess? I froze in place, panicked for a second that I'd been found out. Until I realized he was teasing. I must have been tired. "Haha. I'm flattered you give my feminine charms so much credit. But it was only the first date."

"Only the first? You expect more?" Cody raised his eyebrows.

I shrugged and glanced at my phone, hoping for a text from Mr. Thorne. Or Riggins. Both would be good.

"He hasn't texted you yet?" Cody laughed. "You got it bad! Give him a few hours' sleep, girl. Guys gotta chill before making the next move, you know that."

I put my phone back in my pocket. "I was hoping for a text from the lawyer."

"Oh? Does he work twenty-four hours now? You really are acting like a duchess." He shook his head. "Worried about this newcomer, Lady Something or Other, wanting part of your inheritance? Are you going to have to take it to a jeweler and have them split it in half now?"

Under normal circumstances, everyone in the bakery knew everyone else's business. Now that mine was magnified by the media, my life had become the local entertainment. They all knew about my meeting with Mr. Thorne and the fiction that all I'd inherited was a small piece of jewelry worth a few thousand pounds.

I rolled my eyes. "No idea. I hope she doesn't try to force me to pawn it. I could use the cash, but I don't want to split it with her. Anyway, I'm waiting to hear from Mr. Thorne."

Cody nodded, firmly on my side. "Damn bitch."

On Saturdays and Sundays, we opened at eight and baked more breakfast pastries than during the week. To calm myself, I got in the rhythm, baking coffee cakes, bear claws, cinnamon rolls, and donuts. Looking at the clock every five minutes. Time had never trickled by so slowly. How early did Mr. Thorne get up? When would he check his phone?

Had Riggins heard the news? What was he thinking? Was he already checking Lady Rose out? Had he seen how beautiful Rose was? Would he fall for her instantly? Would he try to buy both of us off? What happened if another female in the line fell out of the woodwork?

I wanted to talk to him. But it was still too early. I couldn't call him this early. And wasn't it bad form for the woman to call first? For either of us to call at all the next day?

Like Cody indicated, someone was supposed to text. My guy friends who were my age endlessly debated how soon a guy should text a woman after a first date. How interested did he want to look? How much relationship power did he want to give up? How much risk of scaring her away did he want to take?

But this was different. I had to know where I stood. First I had to talk to Mr. Thorne to see what the legal ramifications were. Then I needed a lawyer. On Saturday? What about one of those guys you always see on the commercials? *Been in an accident? Call Edwards Law. Don't settle until you talk to us.*

Maybe they were open on Saturdays. An ambulance-chaser marital law/inheritance lawyer? Was there such a thing? I was sinking low. But it wasn't like I had a lawyer on speed dial. And ambulance chasers worked on commission, didn't they? You didn't pay them until you got your settlement?

Just after seven thirty, I was lost in my thoughts, when Steve came back in an agitated state. "Holy shit! Has anyone looked outside? There's a damn crowd out front waiting to get in. With a news crew and some woman decked out in tight jeans, an expensive coat, and heels. She's a looker, I'll tell you that. But what the hell is going on? Since when did a crowd line the side-walk halfway down the street on an ordinary Saturday morning?"

All eyes turned to me.

I gave Steve a panicky look, pulled my phone out of my pocket with a sinking feeling, and pulled up a picture of Rose. "Is this her?" I handed him my phone.

I liked Steve. He'd been with the bakery well before me, for over ten years. He'd been one of their success stories, a help-the-community project. He'd been homeless when the owners hired him and taught him how to bake. He cleaned up his life, got married, had a couple of children, and worked his way up to weekend manager.

Now, here he was giving me a sympathetic look. "That's her."

My pulse roared in my ears. She'd been in London yesterday. She must have hopped the first flight over.

"Who is she?" Steve handed my phone back.

"Lady Rose."

The waitresses—Mary and Stella—and Connie, the cashier, had arrived. I had everyone's attention now.

"Your long-lost relative?" Connie raised an eyebrow. "What does she want? In my experience, long-lost relations always want cash."

"Too bad for her. I don't have any." I shrugged.

"You have something better—a connection to a single billionaire," Stella said.

"Technically, so does she," I said.

Stella shook her head. "Maybe. But I'd watch her."

My coworkers stood in a row, looking like one long scowl. It was heartwarming that they were totally on my side on this one.

Sid thought I should fight. I hadn't thought I'd have to fight at the bakery.

"I wonder what she wants with me *here*?" I said. "She said she wanted to meet her only other living family. But she could have called first."

A low murmur of sympathy and indignation rippled through the bakery.

"She's trying to catch you off guard. Put you in the weak position." Even Mary was on my side. "She shows up here all dolled up—with the press in tow—knowing you'll be in uniform and out of makeup. That's low."

I had a moment of panic. I hadn't even brought my purse with me, just my wallet. I had no makeup on me other than a clear lip balm.

"What you want me to do?" Steve said. "Should I send her away? Tell her you're not in?"

Mary stepped between us. "She's not going to run like a coward." She turned to me. "You have to face this head-on."

Part of me *was* morbidly curious. The other part was furious at her. What did she want—a side-by-side comparison? Something to drive it home to the public just who the beauty was and who was the beastly baker? The gorgeous Brit and the unglamorous Yank?

She had to have gotten hold of the will. She *had* to know we were in a battle for more than a trinket from the late duchess. She must know that millions, a title, and the marriage of the century hung in the balance. The way she'd manipulated the media had to be part of her plan. She was setting herself up as the British contender for duchess.

I was suddenly thankful for Milia's training and makeover. I pulled my hairnet off and shook out my perfectly cut, totally fashionable silvery tresses. "Anyone have some mascara I can borrow?"

Connie gasped. "Your hair is gorgeous!"

Stella stepped forward. "Oh, I have something better, honey! I have a makeup kit in my bag."

Thank goodness for Stella's crush on one of our regulars, Earl. Yeah, the name was ironic now. He wasn't aristocracy like Riggins. He was a trucker. But because of Earl, she kept a healthy supply of makeup on hand to freshen up.

I grinned. "Bring it on!"

When we opened fifteen minutes later, I stood next to Steve as he unlocked the doors. I decided to face Lady Rose as myself, mostly fresh-faced. Just a touch of mascara, some blush, a little photo-ready foundation powder, a bit of pink gloss. Mary and Stella had insisted I wear one of the Blackberry Bakery aprons over my baker's whites. It was tied to show off my figure more than the boxy whites. And why not? With the bakery logo prominently displayed across my chest, the Blackberry would get some free promo. It was the least I owed them for the inconvenience.

But other than that, I was simply myself. Why should I let Lady Rose influence me? Yes, I would fix up for Riggins. But, ultimately, he would have to choose the type of woman who suited him. I refused to be fake. And thanks to Milia and her makeup lesson, I'd done a fair job of applying the natural look in makeup that was so popular. She'd told me to let my hair, which she'd called fabulous, take center stage. I hadn't believed her at first, but it was amazing how much confidence a good cut could give me.

The crush of reporters surged forward, calling my name. Cameras were running. Flashes went off. Standing calmly in front of them all was Lady Rose, smiling, waiting for her cue.

"Haley?" Her face lit up. She pulled me into a ferocious hug. So much for British reserve. Maybe she thought it was the American way.

She smelled like expensive perfume to my vanilla behind the ears. I hadn't wasted my sexy perfume on a workday at the bakery. Mary had been the one to dab me with vanilla and dust me with cinnamon. "The way to a man's heart," she'd said. Never mind the man wasn't in residence right now.

"Cousin!" Lady Rose pulled back and held me by my elbows, taking me in. Or sizing me up.

She was taller than I was. Most people were. She had startlingly large, bright brown eyes that sparkled with good humor. High cheekbones. Full, smiling lips that belonged in a glossy ad for lipstick. The kind of teeth that showed a lot of gum, but were perfectly straight and very white. A pleasant voice highlighted by a cultured accent. Her energy was almost catching.

"This is brilliant. I'm *gobsmacked* to finally meet my real flesh and blood."

To my surprise, she sounded like she actually meant it as she explained who she was and how glad she was to meet me.

She turned me to the cameras with her and leaned down, pressing her cheek against mine. "What do you think? Do you see a family resemblance?" Her teasing laughter was like a tinkling bell over the buzz of speculation around us.

We looked nothing alike. She was a thin, reedy brunette with dark eyes and all the prominent features men liked and women envied. I was like a small, silvery pixie washed in moonlight.

My phone began playing the ringtone I'd set for Mr. Thorne. Of all the bad timing.

CHAPTER THREE

iggins

$\mathcal{R}$ The appearance of Lady Rose changed the game. And not in my favor. If she was authentic, she'd just sealed my fate. I had to marry either her or Haley. The odds were stacked against finding a way to get Lady Rose *and* Haley to refuse to marry me. Staying single was becoming an expensive and dangerous proposition.

I trusted Haley with our secret arrangement. Could I trust Lady Rose? I was beginning to believe Thorne was right—how many more women would pop up and make the claim they were related to the late duchess? Especially if the terms of the will became public?

I pictured the lines to buy lottery tickets when the jackpot got high and knew the answer. I was running out of time.

I had three weeks to get married. If Lady Rose wasn't who she claimed to be, I needed to know *now*. I called my private investigator and got his team on the case. There was no reason I should trust Thorne implicitly.

I wondered, briefly, what the ramifications were for marrying a woman I mistakenly thought fulfilled the terms. Did even Thorne know? Had the Dead Duke considered the scenario? Considering Lady Rose as a candidate for wife was a risky move.

And yet...

Maybe it was the safer play. I couldn't get Haley out of my mind. Couldn't stop aching to see her smile again. To hear her laugh. To taste her lips. It would have been too damn easy to fall for her. Too easy to hurt her in return. To drag both our hearts down a path of no return and no recovery.

Generally, marrying for love was preferred. The problem was time. I had no fucking time. None to find out if this was love. Or lust. Or loneliness. Or just nostalgia.

Maybe it was better to hedge my bets and go for the opportunist I believed Lady Rose to be. No heartaches. Just business. An airtight marriage contract. One heir. We part ways. No messy breakup. Just an amicable divorce. As long as she got her money and her title. And I got an heir and a duchess qualified to be a duchess. One who could teach me the ropes. Raise my son and heir to love his heritage and become the next duke. A duchess who looked like the kind of cool woman I was known for dating. The ice queen whose heart was never in play. The casual fling.

Could a year or more of marriage and a child together be considered a casual fling?

I had a choice. A limited choice, admittedly. But an important choice to make. A chance at love? Risk my heart? Lose my head over a woman? Or a pure business arrangement I could exit unscathed? I drummed my fingers on my desk.

I owed it to myself and the dukedom to check Lady Rose out. Even as I made up my mind to ask her out, I felt like an ass. What would Haley think?

I looked Lady Rose up online. She was everything Thorne had said. Her smile lit up the pages of her social media profiles. She was elegant. Stylish. Damn, she would be a good spokesman for the Flash brand. She had a following. If Lady Rose shopped at Flash, she would influence others to follow. And since our expansion plans had the UK in our crosshairs, that was a point in her favor.

There was also something satisfying to be said about thwarting the Dead Duke's carefully crafted plans.

Lady Rose couldn't be blackmailed by the Dead Duke into marrying me the way Haley could. But from what I saw, I was sure she could be bought. Though I doubted she could be bought out of marrying me.

The question was—how to get in touch with her? Thorne would know. But I had to make it look less calculated. I checked my calendar, thinking I could just

squeeze in a quick trip to the UK. I could take her out.
See where it led. Keep it quiet. If it didn't work out,
Haley would never have to know.

I logged onto one of my social media accounts and
looked her up. Would she accept a friend/follower request from the Duke of Witham? I smiled to myself.
Until a selfie of Haley and Lady Rose together in the
Blackberry Bakery popped up. And I saw it was trending.

Haley was holding a cup of coffee and a donut. Lady
Rose had a cup of tea and a scone. The caption read,
*Me and my American cousin. Aren't we cute?
#longlostrelatives #funfunfun*

Haley

As much as it killed me, I let Mr. Thorne's call go to
voicemail. It wouldn't look good to answer it right in
the middle of this surprise family reunion with the
competition. I could just see myself being pictured as a
self-obsessed bitch who was always on her phone. So I
smiled sweetly for the cameras and went along with
Lady Rose's media blitz.

Did anyone else wonder, like I did, just how genuine
she could be traveling with an entourage of reporters?
And yet at the same time, the horde of reporters
seemed part of who she was. As if she enjoyed them and
couldn't imagine life without them. They were like
breath for her.

"Just pretend they're not here," she whispered to me
in her gorgeous British accent. "Aren't they precious?
They follow me *everywhere*."

To my surprise, they stayed outside when Lady Rose came in.

"They aren't coming in?" I asked.

"Not if they know what's good for them."

I frowned in their direction. "Just how long will they stay out there?"

"Until I leave. But don't worry. They won't bother us."

They already had.

Lady Rose staged us at a table near the window like two stereotypes where the paparazzi could get clear shots of us through the glass. Me with coffee and donuts. Lady Rose with tea and scones.

Personally, I liked tea and scones. Especially our currant scones. And wouldn't have minded having one. But it was a better photo op if we each represented our respective countries' tastes. It would look so much better in an Instagram photo, according to Rose.

"I'm so happy I found you. To have a relative, really!" She touched my arm and beamed.

"But you have a bunch of siblings, don't you?" I said, puzzled by her pleasure.

"Oh, tons, really. My father has been married so many times it's almost scandalous. And he always manages to reproduce with each new wife. Except my mum, of course!" She laughed at her little joke. "But I mean a *blood* relative. Someone who shares my family traits."

I nodded, not having the heart to tell her our blood was very distantly genetically linked. And only if she was genuine.

"I have a sister." I didn't understand Lady Rose's insistence on finding a blood relative. Or how a distantly related stranger like me could add anything to her happiness or sense of wellbeing or belonging.

I told her all about Sid, beaming while I did. I was always proud of my sister. "You'll have to meet her while you're here." What was I doing?

Then I realized I needed Sid's opinion of her. Needed Sid's advice. Needed Sid to win her over and suss her out.

"Of course. Lovely." Lady Rose nodded. She smiled at me, almost sadly. "You don't understand, do you? About me needing to find my bio family?"

I shook my head.

She sighed—beautifully, I might add. Gently dramatic. "My birth mother's dead."

"So's mine."

"But you *knew* her."

I nodded. "But she was also the woman who raised me, and she's gone."

Lady Rose didn't concede my point. There was no way to win an argument with her about this.

"I'm sorry for intruding on your life and surprising you like this. I couldn't help myself. Once I found out about you, I had to meet you immediately. I don't want to be too much of a pain. But I want so badly to get to know you while I'm here."

And maybe horn in on my inheritance?

"How long *are* you here?" I asked.

"As long as it takes! A few days. A week. A month. I'm dying to see Seattle," Lady Rose said. "And visit all the historic spots—where the late duchess lived. The family business. It's still in existence, isn't it?" She sighed. "Isn't this lovely. You and I should go around together! That's a brilliant idea."

I bit my tongue, resisting the urge to ask if the camera crew would be tagging along, too.

As much as I hated to admit it, Lady Rose had natural charisma and charm. She captivated the customers who managed to wedge in to the bakery and stare at us.

The bakery only held forty people maximum. Steve shot me concerned looks. Publicity was good for business. But so were customers. And lack of customers meant losses, not gains.

"I'd love to take you sightseeing," I lied. I would love to escape.

"We should check out the old Wares estate, Wareswood Castle." Her eyes glowed. "Did you know? It's a bed and breakfast now. And wedding venue. You can rent it out for events, obviously. Wouldn't it be fun to poke around it? We might find some clues to the late duchess!"

I had been surprisingly uncurious about Helen. I'd been too busy contemplating an arranged marriage with a billionaire to think much about her. And worrying about Sid.

"A castle? Here in the States! Isn't that delightful?"

"Fascinating."

Apparently Helen had lived like a princess before she became a duchess.

"Yes, a beautiful castle with a striking love story," Lady Rose said, with a dreamy look in her eyes.

I couldn't tell if she was really a romantic, or just faking it. Customers had settled around us and were glomming on to her every word.

"Wareswood Castle, just south of Seattle. It's nestled on a small, private lake on over two hundred acres. The grounds are dotted with old-growth Douglas firs. It was built in 1909 by Helen's lumber baron father for his bride, her mum."

She leaned forward toward me and set her scone down. "But he didn't just build it. He purchased a four-hundred-year-old Elizabethan manor in England. Dismantled it. And had it shipped, brick by brick, to Seattle to be used as the building material for his new Tudor Gothic castle. Which was designed by one of the most famous architects of the day, Kirtland Kelsey Cutter. Isn't that romantic? Wouldn't it be smashing to have a man build a house like that for you?"

I nodded because she seemed to expect it, but my expectations for a home had always been much more modest. And besides, I already owned one with Sid.

Lady Rose smiled, looking almost self-conscious. "Listen to me! I sound like a travelogue. But I haven't told you the best part. The manor Mr. Wares bought in England was one of the country homes belonging to the then-current Duke of Witham's family. He sold it to Mr. Wares to save the dukedom from the rakish ways of his gambler father.

"Isn't it both beautiful and fitting that years later, Helen Wares married the new Duke of Witham and her money again saved it from ruin? It's fate."

Like Rose snagging Riggins for herself and bringing everything full circle? How much did she know? And how could she know it?

Lady Rose was captivating, damn her. And a great storyteller. I sat with my mouth hanging unattractively open while all the patrons of the Blackberry were straining to hear her tale.

She laughed sweetly and demurely, like a true lady, while I cursed myself for not making time to find out more about Helen.

"You must love history," I said, lamely.

"I do. Do you also know that the castle is reportedly haunted?" She nodded, agreeing with herself. "Reportedly by Helen's mum, Grace, who couldn't bear to leave it when she passed because of the love it represented. She's buried on the grounds in sight of the castle. You and I need to go on a ghost hunt. And reassure her all's well with her line today."

At that moment, I didn't think I could convince a living person all was well with me, let alone a ghost.

"*Britain's Got Roots* discovered all this when they traced my ancestry back to Helen's. As my nearest living relative, and hers, I thought you'd want to know."

I was about to say my sister Sid was also her living relative and would like to know, too, when Lady Rose's phone, which sat on the table next to her plate, buzzed. She glanced at it. Her face lit up. "I just received a friend request from our mutual distant relative by marriage, the Duke of Witham." She winked so sweetly and seductively, there was a collective sigh from the diners in the café.

They were Americans! They were supposed to be on *my* side. But apparently the British invasion had begun.

My heart sank. My smile froze on my face as I watched Lady Rose accept Riggins' request. She set the phone down with her long, slim fingers, elegantly manicured.

It had barely touched the table when it buzzed again. She raised a perfectly sculpted eyebrow. "Oh, lovely. He's just PMed me."

I watched in horror as she responded. She'd barely finished typing when her phone nearly simultaneously buzzed with a text. Her smile could only be described as radiant. "The duke would like to take me out to dinner while I'm in town. Is this evening too early?" She gave a sly look toward a camera pointed at us through the window.

Tonight! What was he doing? Hovering by his phone with bated breath waiting for her response. *Crap.*

Lady Rose had just gotten the text I'd been expecting. She, who had no scruples about interrupting our conversation to take a text, had breezed into town and stolen my day-after-a-first-date text in less than half an hour.

I smelled a very clever setup. Lady Rose was obviously a genius at using media to get what she wanted. How would a little introverted amateur like me ever compete with her?

My heart sank. I was losing Riggins already. And the crowd in the bakery, too.

Mary swooped in with a carafe of ice water to refresh our glasses. If looks could kill, Lady Rose would be wet, if not dead. I knew what Mary was thinking—an accidental spill in Lady Rose's beautiful lap would cool her off. But not on camera. Mary couldn't fumble the water in front of the world and give herself and the bakery a bad rep.

As I itched to call Mr. Thorne, I wondered when this media circus would end.

Just as I was about to lose it, the door to the bakery swung open. A florist strode in carrying a long box that usually meant long-stemmed roses. My heart fell all the way to the basement as he headed toward our table. Riggins had been so fast on the getting of Lady Rose's number. Was he equally fast on speed dial to the florist.

Again, there was a collective holding of breath as all eyes and cameras were on the delivery woman. Lady Rose fixed a happy, expectant look of delight on her face. I paled as the florist stopped in front of our table as if she knew exactly what her quarry looked like.

She looked directly at me, ignoring Lady Rose. "Haley Hamilton?"

I nodded.

The florist's smile was bright. "For you."

Stunned, I took the box and opened it. A dozen red roses wrapped in tissue. A card was on top.

Thanks for a wonderful evening. When can I see you again?

Riggins

CHAPTER FOUR

*H*aley
Forget politeness. If Lady Rose could hang on her phone, I could use mine. I wasted no time pulling my phone out and texting him my heartfelt thanks. The paparazzi went wild snapping photos of me beaming with the roses, including Lady Rose.

The roses are beautiful. Thanks. My calendar's open. I hear yours is booked for tonight.

Maybe that was dumb. Or maybe it was a gutsy move. I only knew I had to let him know I had his number.

He texted back. *That's just an obligation. Sunday afternoon? One? I'll pick you up.*

I replied, *Fabulous. It's a date.*

My heart continued to sing, laugh, and soar. He was only seeing Lady Rose out of obligation. I hoped it was true.

My roses upset the lady. Not to mention the rapidly flying texts. Even though I didn't say who to, she knew.

She tried not to let on, but clearly her upper hand had crumbled. She became so flustered, she almost accidentally put my coffee cup into her purse. She would have, in fact, if Mary hadn't startled her and sent the cup crashing to the floor.

The tweets immediately began flying. *Lady Rose rattled as Riggins roses American relative.*

It had nice alliteration, but was the meaning clear?

Mary cleaned up the mess and our table, clearing everything away before Lady Rose could make any more mistakes.

"That woman is a klepto," Mary said after Lady Rose left.

"No, I don't think so. Why would she steal a cheap white ceramic, café-issue coffee cup?" I said. "There's no point. She was just tired."

"I don't trust her." Mary's jaw was set.

"She was perfectly pleasant." My instincts were the same as Mary's. I didn't trust her, either.

Steve let me off early. I wasted no time arranging a meeting with Mr. Thorne as soon as my break ended and Rose left the bakery.

I had no idea what Riggins' game was as I walked into the lobby of Mr. Thorne's hotel, looking for the Englishman. Did Riggins want me? Or want me not? All I knew for sure were that the roses made me ridiculously happy and the symbolism wasn't lost on me. Red roses. Love. Passion. He'd sent me roses and ignored Rose. That had to mean something. At least that we were still allies.

Was he merely continuing the public charade? The fairytale courtship? What about asking Rose to dinner? Merely a friendly gesture? Or checking her out for duchess potential?

The lobby of the downtown hotel where Mr. Thorne was staying was high-end and decorated with glistening surfaces and sparkling crystal chandeliers. I found Mr. Thorne seated in a plush chair, waiting for me.

He stood when I approached. "Miss Hamilton." He extended his arm, offering a chair cozily positioned for conversation opposite him.

"Can we talk freely here?"

Thorne nodded.

I got right to the point. "You know why I'm here. What's this about another heir to the late Helen Feldhem coming forward?" I was unable to think of anything else. "How does this affect me and the terms of the late duke's will?" My heart pounded out of control.

It seemed like lately I was playing game after game of "on the other hand." On the one hand, everything was at stake. On the other, I could be back to where I'd been just over a week ago before I'd ever heard anything about the Dead Duke's death and will. I could go back to normal life. If only I didn't have to worry about Sid. If only I'd never been on a date with Riggins.

Mr. Thorne looked at me kindly. "If her claim is proven and she is, indeed, descended from the late duchess, the duke will be free to chose her as his duchess and all terms will apply."

"If?" I said. "There's some doubt?"

"Her claim was authenticated by a reality television show. Not, perhaps, the most reliable of sources. Particularly since the show's aim is to be sensational and attract viewers.

"My investigators are reviewing her claim and documentation now. But it may take a while. The paper trail is long. And in any ancestral search, the sources can be murky. Making sure the sources are authentic and unaltered is essential and time consuming."

"How long?" I asked.

"Hopefully not longer than three weeks." Mr. Thorne looked sympathetic and almost wry. "There's nothing in the late duke's will that I can find that allows for delays." He paused and cleared his throat. "You could speed the process up considerably."

"Oh?" His statement startled me. "How?"

"By offering up a sample of your DNA. We have no genetic material from the late duchess herself. However, your documentation is sound. We know for a fact that you're descended from Helen Feldhem through her sister, who is your great-grandmother. We could match the genetic markers between you and Lady Rose to see if you are, as she claims, family."

He paused again, almost delicately. "I can't compel you, obviously. The decision is yours."

I frowned, my heart pounding wildly. What to do?

"Would you recommend it?" I sensed an ally in Mr. Thorne or I wouldn't have asked.

"That depends on what you want." His eyes were kind. "As the solicitor for the late duke, it's my responsibility to ask you for a sample. And yet, at the same time, I know you were the late duke's choice of duchess. For more reasons than your DNA."

He stopped himself. "I'm not at liberty to say more. Only that the late duke believed that you will make the perfect Duchess of Witham and be a good match for his successor. If you would have been unsuitable, and the late duke was very particular, even though he believed you were the late duchess' last descendant, he would have abandoned his notion of making one of Helen's descendants the duchess and found someone who was suitable.

"Lady Rose, whatever her basic qualifications may be, was *not* chosen by the late duke, who was a studious and intelligent, thoughtful man.

"If you willingly give us a sample of your DNA, you may put the matter to rest whether her claim is valid. And open yourself up to her as the competition.

"Alternately, you may expose her as an 'unintentional' fraud and put the matter of any contest by her aside. How much risk are you willing to assume? Do you want to take the chance and give her an opening? That decision is ultimately yours and only yours. I would caution you, however, to think through your choices carefully."

I nodded, grateful to Mr. Thorne for his candor. Thankful to have an ally. How much of a gambler was I?

"Is there any way Lady Rose could contest the will and compel me to give DNA?"

Mr. Thorne considered the question. "She may have legal grounds. But that would take time. It's further complicated by the international aspect of the case.

"You could appeal and fight it, stringing it out indefinitely. Longer than three weeks, I would imagine, if you cared to. You have the power, I believe, to force the duke to choose the safer course—you. There's no provision in the will for changing the time restriction."

I nodded, thinking things through. "Does Lady Rose know the terms of the will?" I had my suspicions that she did.

"As far as I know, no. I haven't released the terms to anyone besides you and the duke. Nor have I been approached by any other legal counsel."

We sat in silence a moment as I digested the news.

"I need a lawyer. But I have no idea who to contact. And no money to pay them."

"If you permit, I can make several recommendations. With your financial prospects, you should be able to arrange a payment agreement."

"You mean I find myself an ambulance chaser?" I grinned.

He grinned back. "I believe the correct term is a solicitor who works on contingency."

Riggins

Lady Rose sat across the dinner table from me, looking perfectly put together and gorgeous. Our picture had been snapped roughly three hundred and forty-two times already and we'd hadn't even gotten our water. Appetizers and drinks were still on their way. But who was counting?

She seemed unfazed by the attention. Instead she lapped it up. Talk about extroverted and getting energy from human interaction. What was the word for being energized by social media attention? Besides media whore?

"Having the paparazzi around constantly doesn't bother you?" I stared deeply into her eyes. She definitely handled the press and attention differently than Haley.

Lady Rose shrugged her pale, slim shoulders. "I can't fight them. It only wastes energy being unhappy about them. So why not enjoy them?"

I lifted an eyebrow. "Here in Seattle the press generally respects our privacy."

"What's the fun in that?" Her dark eyes sparkled.

A waiter set two glasses of ice water with lemon in front of us and a glass of wine for Lady Rose, a martini for me.

"So what do I call you?" I asked. "Lady Rose seems too formal. Or am I wrong?"

She laughed again, her beautiful, cultured laugh. "You're a duke. You can call me whatever you like. But Rose will do."

"All right then, Rose." I smiled at her. "And I prefer Riggins, not Duke. Or Witham."

"Now we have that settled." She leaned toward me, staring into my eyes in the candlelight as if hanging on my every word.

"You heard about Haley and hopped on a plane here immediately? Did I get that right? You're impetuous?" I wanted to rattle her. How composed was she? How much of her true intentions would she give away?

"You make that sound like a bad thing." She licked her lips. "Maybe I just know what I want."

Before I could question her further, the waiter appeared to take our order.

Rose turned her luminous eyes on me. "What's good here?"

I'd taken her to a restaurant famed for its Pacific Northwest cuisine. "Anything salmon. You can't go wrong."

She made her selection.

I made mine. The waiter disappeared.

"Before I was interrupted, I was going to ask you what it is you want." I smiled softly at her.

"Very direct." She took a sip of wine, gazing at me over the rim of her glass.

"In my business, I have to be. Isn't it a fair topic for small talk and getting to know each other? Knowing what you want helps me know you."

"Knowing what I want out of life, do you mean?" Her voice was silky, calculatedly so, I decided.

She was polished and charming. She had charisma. She was also hot in her elegant, low-cut, shimmering sheath dress. I should have been completely mesmerized. Why wasn't I? Why was I only *partially* enthralled? And equally leery.

"You tell me. You're the one who brought it up."

There was that seductive smile again. "I'm afraid of wittering on and boring you."

"I very much doubt you could bore me." I gave her my full attention. "I'm easily entertained."

Our appetizers arrived, halting conversation for the moment. When the waiter left again, Rose delicately plucked a crab cake from the plate in the center of table, dipped it in aioli, and glanced around the room.

"You're an observant, intelligent man. I believe you *know* what I want, Riggins. Why I hurried here." She set her appetizer fork down and leaned forward toward me, intimately lowering her voice. "It's no secret—I want to be your duchess."

I stared at her. "Am I supposed to be shocked by your frank admission?"

"Not at all. I believe in being direct."

"You're putting yourself out there as the first British candidate for the job?"

"I'm highly qualified. And I have the backing of a nation behind me."

I nodded. "A plane full of aspiring duchesses is arriving from Britain on Monday. I'll soon have my choice of hundreds of hopefuls." Was she just another opportunist? Or did she know how potentially eminently qualified she was?

"None of them have the vital qualification I do." She paused, looking me in the eye. "I believe we both know what I'm talking about."

She was being mysterious. I didn't want to tip my hand. She could be referring to her rearing and aristocratic status.

"I hope you don't believe everything you hear in the news? To the contrary, I'm in no rush to marry and procreate, as they seem to believe."

"I wouldn't believe something as unreliable as the tabloids." There was that smile again and the forward lean. She took my hand where it rested on the table and looked me intimately in the eye as she stroked the side of my hand with her thumb. "I know all about the will, Riggins. *All* about it. *Every* detail."

I kept my composure, keeping my expression masked. "Do you? Enlighten me."

She held my gaze. "Not here. The walls have ears. In private."

She slid her foot between mine beneath the table and lifted the hem of my slacks with the toe of her shoe, still smiling. "I'll give you my terms. I want to do everything I can to make you happy...with your deal. But first, let's enjoy our dinner and get to know each other. We're almost family, really."

"All right, then," I said. "After-dinner drinks are at my place."

Haley

There was one good and, at the same time, horribly bad thing about Riggins' and Rose's celebrity status. I could spy on them without leaving the comfort of wherever I wanted to be. All I needed was my phone and my social media apps.

As it turned out, I *was* at home. Watching TV with Sid. With my bouquet of red roses on the stand next to me to remind me that Riggins wanted to see me again.

Sid and I had gone over and over all the possible meanings of the roses. And my conversation with Mr. Thorne.

"No DNA. Don't give her that. No way! Not if you want him. Not if you want that lifestyle." Sid was adamant. Fierce to the point her eyes flashed and her voice rose.

Fortunately, our roomies were out for the evening, so we could talk freely.

"But isn't it only fair and right?" I said, once again playing the righteous good girl. "Shouldn't Riggins have the choice, if there is one? How would I feel knowing I'd tricked him into marriage by denying him the chance with Rose? Maybe the two of them will be perfect together. She's much better suited to that life than I am. Do you see how gorgeous they look together—"

Sid shook her head. "No way. Just *no.* Do you want to hand him over to a gold digger? And how is it tricking him into marriage when the Dead Duke forced you into this situation in the first place? Nothing you could do could be called trickery."

I shrugged. She made a good point.

"If the situation was reversed, don't you think Lady Rose would do everything in her power to keep you from being a contender?"

"But I'm not her. I have to do what's right."

"But what's right in this situation, Hale? Seriously, where's the moral high ground here and why pursue it?"

I sighed.

"And what about Lady Rose and her accidental kleptomania at the Blackberry?" Sid touched my arm. "You want to know what I think? She was trying to steal the cup to get your DNA.

"She tricked you into having coffee with her and it was just her bad luck you didn't choose a paper cup she could steal. They do it all the time on the cop shows—trick a crook into drinking a cup of coffee and tossing it away for them to steal and mine for DNA."

I had considered that, actually. "The thought crossed my mind."

Sid nodded, vehement. "Exactly. She's playing hardball while acting all sweet and sentimental. See how quickly she got a dinner invitation with Riggins? All of this is anything but accidental. She's a cold, calculating bitch."

Sid tightened her grip on my arm. "You have to be careful, very careful around her. She's a DNA thief. If she gets a chance, she'll steal yours. All she needs are a few strands of your hair or a bit of your saliva on something. Watch yourself, Hale. Stay away from her."

I nodded. "Maybe you're right—"

"Of course I am!" She hugged me. "Now get over your guilt and resign yourself to protecting Riggins and his dukedom from the clutches of a conniving woman. In the meantime—duchess lessons!"

Sid had become addicted to the idea of me being the duchess. "I found some excellent shows on Netflix about manor houses in England and Scotland. They interview the aristocratic families still living there. We can learn a lot from them!"

She was so excited. And I was curious. We settled in to watch the shows. What kind of life would I be in for as a modern-day duchess? The reality as explained by the living earls and dukes was very different from the pampered past when servants attended to the lord's every need. As they explained it, economies must be made and the estates run as businesses. One of the duchesses occasionally even groomed her own horse and mucked her own stall.

I jealously checked my phone every five minutes, which Sid, surprisingly, seemed to approve of. Just after eleven, a picture of Riggins pulling into the long, gated driveway of his lakefront mansion with Rose in the passenger seat popped up on my feed.

"He took her home!" My voice broke. I both saw red and was on the verge of hysterical tears.

Sid glanced at her watch. "Eleven? That's good. The evening is ending early." She sniggered.

"No. I meant to *his* home." I handed her my phone.

"Oh." Her face fell.

Crap. He hadn't taken *me* home. We both knew what that meant.

Riggins

Rose's eyes were large as she took in my home and the view over the dark water sparkling with the reflection of the city and surroundings. She was impressed. But she studied it with the eye of a woman used to luxury and quality.

"Beautiful." She looked around and up the grand staircase. At the paintings and light fixtures. Appraising them or enjoying them?

"Thank you." I took her coat and showed her to the living room where the view was most spectacular and I almost never closed the curtains and blinds. "You should see the view in the daylight. Can I get you anything?"

"Thank you. A glass of wine? Something dry. I'm still stinging from that rich dessert." She settled into the plush upholstery of my favorite sofa and kicked off her shoes.

"I have just the thing." I poured her a glass of Riesling, handed it to her, and took a seat in the chair at a right angle to her.

"Your tastes are very modern and yet classic. With definite Northwest elements thrown in." She picked up a small black statue of swimming salmon that sat on the end table next to her. "It's refreshing after growing up in a museum like I have."

I smiled at her. "Some would say you've been lucky."

She shrugged and set the statue down. "They haven't lived among antiquity. They're spoiled with modern conveniences like electric wiring that isn't wonky."

She laughed prettily. "I read stories about people here in America renovating 'old' houses. Those built in nineteen hundred, for example. And all the tribulations they have bringing them up to code without destroying the historic character of them.

"Imagine trying to keep a three-hundred-year-old manor house looking essentially the same as it did in

1816, including the furnishings. Yet having Wi-Fi and satellite TV. Computers sitting around. That kind of thing. It would be so nice just to start from new with twenty-first-century style."

"You're a modern girl?" I said.

"I am what I have to be." Her smile was dazzling, but beneath it there was a hint of frustration.

The evening had been a success. I'd had a good time. And she certainly knew how to be mysterious. But the time had come for revelations. She'd been coming on to me all evening. Under ordinary circumstances, I wouldn't have discouraged her. But given what was at stake, I preferred to take things slow. Complicating things, Haley kept popping into my thoughts at the most awkward, inconvenient times.

"You were going to tell me all about the contents of the Dead Duke's will." I wanted to see if she was fishing or if she really knew what she was talking about.

"The Dead Duke?" She laughed. "Is that what you call him? Brilliant! I love it. He was such an old codger. Not that I, or anyone, ever saw much of him. My father, of course, had dealings with him from time to time and paid the odd social call. But I suppose the old duke deserves the name. He *is* very dead. Probably had been for years, though he breathed on in that ancient, dried-up body of his."

"You're more sentimental about him than I am." I grinned. "I never met him." I raised my glass. "To the Dead Duke. May he rest in peace."

We clinked glasses.

Rose laughed again. "Oh, he won't be resting in peace anytime soon. He'll be turning in his grave if he ever hears about my plans."

She paused and wrapped her hands around the stem of her wine glass. "I know many of the details of the will. I'm not supposed to, obviously, but I have friends in low and medium places. Servants and clerks to the Dead Duke. People who were invisible to him, but who knew what to look for and liked to talk and speculate.

"Although there were rumors the old duke was probably immortal, I realized he couldn't live forever. Eventually there would be a new duke. I've been keeping tabs to see who that would be. To my great satisfaction, that was you." Her eyes danced. Her voice was full of flirt.

"There's a shocking lack of eligible dukes on the market. And a desperate shortage of rich, handsome, *young* dukes. When a new one pops up, the sharks will circle. A girl needs to be prepared. If she wants to be a duchess, that is. The only way is to marry into the title. So, yes, I have been spying on the Dead Duke, looking for any advantage with his heir." She laughed. "Does that sound terribly conniving and scheming of me?"

"It has a certain Mata Hari ring to it." I leaned back in my chair. "Others might say it was prudent. Wise, even."

She laughed and smiled at me as she took another sip of wine and crossed her legs. "You see? You and I could get on famously."

I nodded. "You were saying?"

"The Dead Duke was a well-known manipulator. That's no secret. He also made it clear his dynasty was the most important thing to him. Everyone in his social circles and in our little community was aware of his aspirations. He wanted an heir and an heir for his heir.

"If I don't miss my guess—and judging from your expression, I don't—he's implemented a plan for ensuring your compliance with his wishes. The late duke was very clever. Practically diabolical." Her eyes sparkled.

She leaned on the arm of the sofa so that her cleavage showed to full advantage and smiled into my eyes seductively. "Imagine my great pleasure when the new duke was *everything* I'd been hoping for."

I raised an eyebrow and smiled, encouraging her with my silence to continue.

"An opportunity like this only comes around once in a lifetime. Coincidentally—it must have been fate—I was on the show *Britain's Got Roots* and discovered my connection to his late first wife." She took another sip of wine. "He's reputed to have had an exceptional love for her. As evidenced by leaving her only living female relative something in his will. That wasn't like him at all."

I wondered just how coincidental that revelation was. Or if it had been manufactured. Could she have faked her ancestry? Her good fortune seemed a little *too* convenient. And just how much did she really know?

"The Dead Duke is most likely blackmailing you into taking the dukedom somehow. You don't seem the kind to be eager to take it over. You're smart enough to realize what an albatross it could be. Without some incentive to marry and take it over, you're rich enough to refuse.

"And, from what I've observed, I'm willing to wager that he wants you to marry a descendant of his first wife. He believed only Haley Hamilton remained of the late duchess' line. But he was wrong, the old fool. I'm one, too. Thank you, *Britain's Got Roots.*" She paused, studying me.

"I have no scruples about marrying you. For your money. For fun. So we both get what we want." She leaned toward me. "You're a bit of all right. Life with you could be loads of fun. Especially if we go into this honestly with no false expectations." She took a sip of wine.

I masked my expression. "You're fully aware of all the requirements of a duchess?"

"You're referring to having to produce an heir?" She laughed. "Yes. Oh, yes. I'm perfectly willing to populate your dukedom with a lovely, handsome son. And maybe a spare. If your Dead Duke's will is like many contracts in wealthy old families, there's a bonus for that, too. He was a traditionalist, so I don't believe my guess is far off." She took my hand and made bedroom eyes at me. "That's the fun bit of this whole arrangement, isn't it?"

My mouth went dry. She *was* enticing.

"I would suggest we up our odds of conceiving a boy the first time out and you pay for a tummy tuck after we've had our beautiful little heir and spare. I don't believe either of us want to have six or eight girls trying for a boy. That's way too much stress."

I laughed, not sure whether I was horrified or impressed with her honesty and forthrightness. "Hardly."

"I'm fertile. I've been checked out. I can give you my medical records."

"I—"

She waved her hand. "Oh, don't worry about it or be embarrassed. It's only sensible. Were I in your shoes, I'd do the same.

"One of my spies claims she heard whispers that the will calls for a pregnancy test before the marriage. The bride must not be pregnant before, even with your child. The Dead Duke"—she laughed—"didn't want any usurpers to his genetic line taking the dukedom. I don't disbelieve it. It would be completely in character.

"I'm happy to take the test on our wedding day. And after the children are born, if we decide to part, I'll give you custody and only ask for visitation rights. I promise to show the proper amount of affection and attention as their mum. And raise the eldest son to be a good little duke. As long as I'm guaranteed my bonus for producing the heir.

"I'll play your loving wife in public. Your passionate wife in the bedroom. We could have so much fun. And the divorce, should we decide to divorce at the conclusion of our contract, will be amicable.

"During our marriage, I won't embarrass you. I'll introduce you to society. And teach you how to be an aristocrat. All in all, we could have a lovely life together, you and I. For as long as it lasts.

"We'll spell everything out in writing beforehand so we both know what we're getting into and what our legal rights are."

I remained silent. She was logical and organized. Astute and conniving. Passionate, but a little calculatingly cold at the same time. On the surface, she was exactly everything I needed. But was she what I *wanted*?

We certainly didn't need this leak. I needed to call Thorne and let him know we had a problem.

"You must think I'm very cold and calculating. That I love money above all else." She smiled sadly. "The truth is, I'm more like the Dead Duke than I like to admit. You no doubt know my father is on the brink of losing our ancestral home? I know I'm only adopted, but I have strong family ties. I couldn't bear for him to lose it and for our family to lose its prestige.

"Part of the reason I'm doing this is for my family. To save everything."

CHAPTER FIVE

aley
Sunday was clear and warm for January—fifty degrees. Riggins invited me to his house for our date and sent a car to pick me up. He told me to dress casually, but bring a warm jacket.

His house sat on the beach down a long, gated driveway from the road. If the definition of luxury is privacy and plenty of space, he was definitely living the life. The car had to be buzzed in through security.

As I watched the wrought-iron gate swing open, my heart raced at the thought of seeing him again. There was an instant where I wondered if I could stand a life where living behind a gate was necessary. Where security was a prime concern and you didn't just walk out to the mailbox and chat with your neighbors. There was freedom in being an ordinary person with an ordinary income. How much of that was I willing to give up for love of my sister, and maybe just love period?

Despite all my misgivings, I couldn't help smiling at the thought of seeing Riggins. There was no denying I was attracted to him and falling in love with him. But that was such dangerous ground, loving a man who might never love me. Trying to get him to marry me to save Sid and save him from Lady Rose's diabolical clutches. Yes, I was often melodramatic. But there you had it. Thinking of him with Lady Rose broke my heart. Thinking of him with anyone but me did.

I texted Riggins that I had arrived. He was waiting for me in front of his home as we pulled up. Waterfront property on Lake Washington was at a premium and exceptionally pricey. The sheer number of lakefront footage he had was almost dizzying when I considered what it must have cost. The non-lakeside of his house was attractive, but not ostentatious.

Dressed in jeans and a casual jacket, Riggins, however, was nothing short of hot. His face lit up when he saw my car pull up. I couldn't help beaming.

He opened the car door for me. I had to resist flying into his arms as if he were mine and this fairytale courtship was something more than a plot to throw Thorne off. Riggins smelled delicious, as always, of virility mixed with amber, mint, cedarwood, and citrus, and wore a day's growth of beard that highlighted the impression of natural, sexy masculinity. But it was the delight in his eyes at seeing me that took my breath away. I could live in that look for the rest of my life. If only he'd let me.

"Haley!" He pulled me into a tight hug, clasping me to his hard chest in a natural embrace.

When our eyes met, a spark leaped between us. The intimacy of a night of dancing hadn't faded.

He took my hand. "Come on. Let me show you the house. After the tour, I have something special planned. I hope you like the water?"

I raised an eyebrow. "You aren't planning to throw me in, are you?"

He laughed. "Hardly."

"In that case, I love the water."

He pulled me into the entryway of the house. I resisted gaping only with supreme effort. The house was as breathtaking as the man who owned it.

"It's beautiful!" I was in true awe.

His tastes were a mix of classic and modern. Very elegant. The house even smelled expensive. It was *not* your typical bachelor place. Every surface sparkled as if it was polished and dusted regularly. There were definitely no dirty socks lying around.

"Not too masculine?" he asked.

"Not for you," I said truthfully.

The focus of the house was the lakeside. A wall of windows so clean it almost felt open-air ran the length of the living room. Which had a view of the lake and the Olympic Mountains that could only be described as killer. "Look at that view." I took a step forward, tugging him with me. "I feel like I could see forever to the mountains and beyond."

He looked at me with a strange expression. "That's exactly how I feel. It's what sold me on the house. But you're the first person who's ever said it to me."

I smiled at him. *See? Soulmates,* I wanted to say. *Priceless.*

He had an expanse of lush green lawn that led to the lake.

I ran with my thoughts, not filtering them. "Do you ever run barefoot through that lush lawn to the lake in the evening when the shadows are long? And get that ache from the cold. I love running through cold grass at dusk. Yours looks so thick I just want to curl my toes in it."

"Not this time of year." He was looking at me like I had once again voiced his thoughts. "You have to watch out for banana slugs."

I laughed.

He had a boathouse and a dock that appeared as large as one at the public park in Renton. And moored at it was a sleek white yacht that looked like something from a Bond movie.

"Well?" He squeezed my hand. "First impressions?"

"Wow." I took a deep breath. "That's all I have—just wow! I feel like I've stepped into an episode from HGTV. One where they showcase the homes of the rich and famous."

"I am rich." He winked.

I laughed. "Don't forget famous, now that you're the duke."

He grimaced. "Don't remind me. Let me show you the rest of the main floor."

He could have released my hand, but he didn't. I tried not to read too much meaning into it. My hand in his felt so natural, maybe he simply forgot. Maybe he held every girl's hand. Maybe he didn't want to take a chance I'd go running wild through the house pulling open doors and marveling at the wonders inside.

He took me around, showing me one spectacular room after another. Introducing me to his staff, including his housekeeper, who lived in a "cottage"—which was nicer than my house—on the property.

At one point, I stopped short to admire a piece of art and looked him in the eye. "You live like this. And yet you're afraid you don't know how to be a duke? How is this different? I bet you live better than most modern-day dukes.

"Sid and I have been watching specials about the great estates of England and Scotland on Netflix. As far as luxury? You have them beat. Most of the earls and dukes on those shows run tourist shops on their properties, wield chainsaws to clear trees that fall over their private roads, and use backhoes to store biofuel to save on energy costs.

"The Duke of Argyll even tends shop and wears an apron that says 'Duke' on it. And he's the head of the entire Campbell clan worldwide!" I squeezed Riggins' hand. "When was the last time you clerked at a store?"

"I manned the cash register at one of our charity sample sales." His smile was breathtaking. "And I wore a bright blue volunteer apron during my stint."

"But did it say 'duke' on it?" I teased.

"I wasn't the duke yet."

"Technicality. How about 'boss'?"

He laughed. "No. But back to your original question—do you see any five-hundred-year-old paintings of my ancestors painted by famous masters hanging on the walls?" He shuddered, playfully. "The thought of all those eyes following me gives me nightmares. And stuffed deer heads in the drawing room? Dusty old books in the library? I hate dust and the smell of old." He shook his head.

"Elizabethan isn't your style?" I teased.

"No, not even the much more recent Victorian. Come. Let me show you my theater."

The theater room was also marvelous and seated about thirty in ultra-comfy seats. I tried every one while he laughed.

"Not a bad seat in the house," I finally pronounced.

He also had an office, a private gym, an indoor pool, an outdoor pool, a spa room, a game room, a man cave, and a bar. He had basically everything.

"Why do you ever leave this house even for a moment?" I asked as I stood next to him, our shoulders almost brushing. "It's like a self-contained city unto itself."

"Well, there's the lake—"

"All right. I'll give you that." I smiled at him.

"And I have to earn a living." He sounded so endearingly earnest. Like he was just a normal guy with a nine-to-five job driving a truck or something.

I laughed. "No, all you really have to do for the rest of your life is count your money and watch it grow. Almost literally, you could spend the rest of your life counting your money. I've been trying to wrap my head around the concept of a billion. Of knowing a billionaire. Of you being a billionaire and having a billion dollars.

"I Googled it—it would take you almost thirty-two years just to count to a billion. That's just to *one* billion.

"According to the Rule of 72, if you invested at a modest interest rate of even just two percent, by the time you reached the end of your thirty-two years of counting, you'd have almost another billion. And have to keep counting. By the time you reached the end again, your money would have doubled again. You could keep counting your money literally forever."

He raised both eyebrows and pursed his lips. "I've never thought of that. Astonishing. But a waste of time. I pay accountants to do it for me."

I grinned. "I'm not done with my deep thinking. Even if you do nothing and earn a paltry one percent per year, no compounding, that's..."

I bit my lip as I did the math in my head. "Ten million dollars?" I nodded. "Yes, ten million dollars. And you have more than one billion, at least according to *Forbes*. And you certainly make more than one percent per year. Unless something catastrophic happens"—we both knew what that was—"you won't be able to spend your money in your lifetime."

"I do love a girl with a head for math," he said tenderly. "And an inquisitive mind, especially when I'm the subject."

"I need to know what I'm *potentially* getting into." I was dying to ask him about Lady Rose. And fighting constant jealousy when my thoughts came anywhere near him giving her this tour.

He'd taken her here. Before me. Had he impressed her with his wealth and sense of style? Tantalized her with the lifestyle she could lead, at least for a while, if she won his affection?

I looked at him again and said, sincerely, "Am I supposed to be impressed by all this? What do you want from me?"

"If you're not impressed by this, you're impossible to please." He grinned, clearly teasing, but watching me closely.

I shrugged. "Maybe I'm not a material girl. Maybe I'm only impressed with deeper, intangible things."

He stopped short. "Like what?"

"Love. Loyalty. Character. Honesty."

"Then I'll have to work hard."

"Don't work hard. Just be you," I said. "You're pretty astonishing all on your own." I leaned in and whispered in his ear. "I'd like you even if you weren't rich and titled. And I wasn't being forced to marry you, maybe. Unless we defeat the dastardly Dead Duke."

His smile deepened.

I rested my head on his shoulder, playfully. "Is this the date we'll remember fifty years from now on our golden anniversary? Figuratively speaking, of course."

He just smiled. "Maybe. Depends on how good your memory is."

I laughed and pulled my head away from his shoulder. "Here's the ten-million-dollar question, again, quite literally—how are the getting-out-of-a-wedding plans coming? Is there a potential golden anniversary? Or even a paper anniversary in our future? Should I be shopping for a dress?"

It was dumb, maybe, to ask. And to ruin the playful, flirty mood. But I had to know where things stood. I wasn't good at standing in limbo.

He ran his fingers through my hair, rubbing it in his fingers. "You're thinking of Lady Rose."

His touch sent shivers up my spine. I ached for him, I realized with a start. I would tumble into bed with him in an instant just to be with him, even if I was afraid my inexperience would show. But I didn't want to be just another billionaire groupie.

"She's the invisible wall here, isn't she?" I fought to keep my voice steady. "The elephant in the room. The fly in the ointment. The complication. The disease infecting a perfect plan."

We were all alone. No staff in sight. I felt I could ask without anyone else hearing.

"A disease!" He laughed at that and sighed. "Cruel. But not far off the mark. Yes, she is *the* complication."

He paused and became serious. "With her in the picture, and no way yet to thwart the Dead Duke's plans, I'll probably have to marry one of you. I'm sorry. I don't mean to string you along. I need to make sure I make the right decision."

"Every man deserves that. Choosing a wife, even with a great selection of two women, is an important decision." I swallowed hard. "What about your promise to help Sid?"

He looked surprised. "I gave you my word. No matter what happens, I'll do everything I can to help Sid."

I smiled and nodded. "Okay, then, you've just impressed me. Best date ever, already. Just remember—I'll hold you to your promise."

He grinned. "Can we forget about Rose now and enjoy the day?"

"Absolutely! I'm all for it. What do you have planned?" I bumped him playfully, coming up against his rock-hard bicep.

"Come on. I'll show you. Bring your jacket." He pulled me by the hand out of the house through the glass doors toward the lake. Right to that big-ass Bond boat yacht thing.

"Up for a little boating?" He grinned.

"A *little* boating?" I laughed. "What's wrong? Is your ocean liner in the shop?"

He laughed. "I'm pulling out all the stops to impress you."

"A ride on your yacht is the price of my silence?" I walked with him to the dock, enjoying the feel of the mild day and being so near him.

The captain welcomed us aboard. Riggins led me to the main deck, where drinks and appetizers waited for us.

"Why do I feel like I'm in an episode of *The Bachelor*?"

"Is that what this is?" He laughed. "Did Jennifer make a deal for one of those shows I've been pitched behind my back?"

"What shows?"

He handed me a drink. "*The Bachelor Duke*, British and American version. I think that was one they were pitching."

"You're kidding?" I said.

"Sadly not." He sighed. "Twelve gorgeous Americans and twelve British aristocrats vie for the title of duchess. Who will I hand a tiara to?"

I shook my head. "I suppose one American baker and one British earl's daughter, and a plane full of British hopefuls, is enough for one guy to handle. Oh. Wait. That sounds an awful lot like—"

He laughed again. "Stop. Maybe the producers are right. Maybe I should have signed on. It's this damn time limit that's stopping me up." He passed me a plate of delicious-looking salmon puffs and sat down next to me, thigh to thigh as a gentle breeze ruffled his hair.

In the sunlight, with the wind playing with his hair, it was all I could do not to sigh and keep my hands off him. He was hot. But much more than that, I liked him. I was falling in love with him and had all the giddy, passionate emotions falling in love comes with.

The not being able to keep my eyes off him. The wanting to know everything about him and thinking every little thing was special and unique. I wanted to find out and marvel over all we had in common. And be thrilled at all the exciting things he did that were different from what I did. I wanted to impress him by try-

ing to fit into his life and try the things he liked. I
wanted to be able to sit in companionable silence with
him and just be. I wanted to touch and touch and touch
him and never part.

My heart sighed. My pulse raced. I had never felt
anything before like this, absolute joy at just being
with him.

And absolute terror at what that meant.

The yacht pulled away from the dock and began a
slow cruise just out from the shore. I had cruised the
lake before with friends and on a cruise once in college.
The houses along the lake were fantasies, dream homes
I could never aspire to. Well, until now. Maybe.

I tried to picture myself actually living in Riggins'
mansion and almost laughed aloud. It was so ridiculous.
Like a dream that would be snatched away when I
woke.

Cruising with Riggins was an altogether different
experience than my previous jaunts around the lake.
There was no dry cruise director pointing out houses of
the rich and famous and reciting canned details. No
group of regular people oohing and aahing over the
houses and speculating how much money you'd have to
have to afford one.

To Riggins, the houses along the lake were the
homes of his friends and acquaintances. He'd been to
parties and social gatherings at too many of them to
count. And he had anecdotes and stories to tell about
them. Intimate stories that made me laugh. Salacious
stories about mistresses and wives almost meeting up.

Forbidden lovers. Love triangles. Ordinary stories, just details about his friends.

"That one"—he pointed to an Italianate mansion— "is my partner Justin's place."

I had been eyeing it, actually. "It's beautiful. I think it's my favorite. Next to yours, of course."

Riggins nodded and pointed to a second-floor window. "His wife has been decorating the nursery. They're expecting their first baby in March. The pregnancy has been good for Flash. Jus' wife Kayla has complained about finding unique, boutique baby clothes, accessories, and furniture. Because of her experiences, we've expanded into baby products and business is booming.

"I'll have to introduce you to Jus and Kayla. You'd love them."

When you're falling in love, little things are thrilling. You find meaning in everything. *He wants me to meet his friends! He's planning a long-term future together.*

"If I pass the duchess test and you can't find a way to wriggle out of marriage?" I whispered to him.

He laughed and pointed to another house without answering my question. "That one belongs to Old Lady Diamond. She's a retired software exec and the lake's original lonely cat lady. She was one of the original programmers at one of Seattle's earliest software giants. People say she was a brilliant programmer. But she's a little odd." He made a circle motion around his head.

"If you ever have the misfortune to be asked to dine at her home—don't eat anything. She's notoriously cheap. Half the food is day-old and stale and the cats are all over the table and everything.

"She's filthy rich, but she saves all of her scraps of bar soap. She's a classic hoarder. The house, however, is worth seeing. It's an ode to 1988. I don't think she's bought a new piece of furniture since then. If you like oak furniture, score."

As we cruised leisurely around the lake, Riggins opened a bottle of champagne that had been chilling in a bucket. He used a fancy gas-powered cork remover. The cork came out just fine. But the champagne bubbled out onto the deck of the boat and all over Riggins' lap. He jumped up and held the bottle over the edge, spilling champagne into the lake.

He turned to me. "That was smooth."

I started laughing. On impulse, I grabbed the glasses, stood, and held them out for him to fill. "This wouldn't happen if you just drank beer like regular people."

"What?"

"Yeah. When you cruise the lake, beer is the traditional drink of choice. Screw-top is fine."

"I like beer. I'm trying to impress you with this three-hundred-dollar bottle of champagne I just fed to the fish."

"There you go again, throwing figures around." I leaned up against the rail next to him and stared into the dark water. "Impress me with a good-quality IPA. I'd be fine with that."

I took a sip of champagne. "But this is heavenly. Just I feel like I should be at a wedding or special occasion."

"Being out with you is a special occasion," he said.

"You say the sweetest things." I swallowed a lump in my throat. "Where are we going?"

"To a place I can get to know you better."

"Ah. Mysterious." I pointed. "It looks like we're headed for the Montlake Cut. Which could mean Seattle. Or the arboretum. The lakeside rec center. Or possibly even the University of Washington."

He shrugged. "My lips are sealed. You'll find out soon enough."

I looked back at the dark water and shivered as a gust of wind rippled the lake.

"Cold?" He put his jacket around my shoulders.

"I'd love to see the rest of the yacht."

"Sure."

The yacht was as fabulous as his house. I told him so. "Now it's a tossup. I can't decide whether you should live on the yacht or in the house. Maybe divide your time."

He laughed. Soon we were mooring next to the rec center.

I turned a curious gaze on him. "You're taking me to our alma mater?"

"Common ground. I want to know everything about you. I figured this was a good way to start the conversation."

We walked around the University of Washington, stopping for a cup of coffee in a trendy little coffee shop just off campus.

On our first real date, we'd made small talk and felt comfortable with each other. Now we talked and talked and talked. About our majors, our hopes, and dreams.

Riggins had gone to the U and graduated in business. He'd been in a frat, mostly to have a community at the large, often overwhelming and impersonal school. Nearly forty-five thousand students attended class at the U's campus in the heart of the city. A large percent of them commuters. I'd been one of them. Finding your tribe was essential.

I pointed out the buildings where I'd had class. And my favorite spots to study and dream. We walked through Red Square, peeked into the library, which reminded me of an old British library or a cathedral, the kind of library you'd imagine a wizard attending. I showed him my favorite spot to study. He showed me his.

We walked to Drumheller Fountain with its spectacular view of Mt. Rainier. The fountain and the green behind it were designed to point right at the mountain for the 1909 Alaska-Yukon-Pacific Exposition.

We took a selfie with Mt. Rainier in the background. He pulled me into a delicious kiss.

"I wish I'd had a boyfriend like you when I was in college." I laughed at myself.

"Is that what I am?"

"A fake one, anyway," I said.

"That's no kind of boyfriend to have." He tipped my chin up and kissed the end of my nose. "I wish I'd had a girlfriend like you in college—a cute one."

"Cute?" I laughed.

"Stunning. Fun. You're beautiful."

"I wasn't fishing—"

He kissed me again and took my hand. We walked hand in hand back to the yacht.

"That was beautiful. Just like being in college again. How is that we've avoided the paparazzi?" I asked.

"We didn't." He pointed toward a man at a distance on shore as he helped me aboard. "They were following us at a distance. Ten to one that kiss is already sold to a tabloid somewhere."

I followed where he pointed. "Is that why you made it so delicious?"

He grinned.

"At least they're keeping their distance. That's an improvement."

"Yeah." He kissed me again.

The yacht was staffed with a steward as well as the captain. The steward greeted us. "Which deck would you like to have dinner on this evening, sir?"

"The lower deck," Riggins said.

I laughed. "Well, isn't that pretentious? Which deck?"

Riggins grinned. "Not pretentious. With three decks, practical. Come on. We still have to cruise Lake Union before sunset."

He led me to the lower deck, where we sat side by side as we cruised Lake Union with its fabulous view of Seattle.

"Should we try to find the houseboat they used in *Sleepless in Seattle*?" Riggins asked. "It's one of the lake's claims to fame."

"You know that movie was made the year I was born?" I said.

He nodded. "Was it?"

I shook my head. "You knew!"

"Why do you think I picked it?" He laughed and signaled the captain. "You have seen it?"

"Once. Part of it, anyway. On TV. I'm not even sure what that houseboat looks like."

Riggins brought up a picture on his phone. "This look familiar?"

"Not at all. But I'm up for a game of where's the houseboat."

After much debate about which one it was, exactly, we found it. I had the feeling the captain had known where it was all along.

Riggins signaled the captain to head back. The shadows were long and the air became crisp, ruffling my hair as we cruised. But wrapped in Riggins' arms beneath the heaters on the deck, I was warm and happy.

The afternoon had been like a dream. As we cruised through the Montlake Cut back into Lake Washington, the sun slanted over the water, getting ready to set.

"All right. So maybe this is a date we'll always remember," I said. "I'll always remember, anyway. Maybe it's standard operating procedure for you to take women out on the boat."

He nuzzled my neck. "Only the special ones."

"You mean duchess material."

"Yeah, and not even all of those."

Why did that admission make my heart sing? He hadn't taken Lady Rose on the yacht. For the last twenty-four hours I'd suffered through the media fawning over her and speculating about her date with Riggins. But he hadn't taken her on the yacht, which was clearly special to him, his baby. So maybe she wasn't so special after all.

We were alone on the deck. As the sun set, he pulled me onto his lap.

I wrapped my arms around his neck and pressed my forehead to his. "Duke, this has been an amazing day."

The tip of my nose touched the tip of his as we stared into each other's eyes. He put his hand behind my neck. I lowered my lips to his. It was just a light brush of a kiss, lips barely meeting. A tease. But it took my breath away.

One tiny kiss. And then another. I tilted my head and parted my lips. He gently sucked my lower lip as I ran my fingers through his hair. Another kiss. A little deeper this time. A tantalizing flicker of tongue. My heart raced. My breath became shallow. I felt the power of his soft, romantic kisses all the way to my core.

I slid around until I was straddling him and looking down at him. I could look at him all day long, all my life long. If he'd only been just a regular guy. And we'd had time to take our time and fall in love at a natural pace. Not that I seemed to need much time. My heart was already racing toward his. It wanted him. I wanted him. I kissed him, letting go. Showing him how much.

Our kisses grew deeper. He slid his hands beneath my sweater, burning my skin with his hot grip. We necked like two teenagers desperate for each other. I was desperate for him, anyway. And trying not to think. Because this could only lead to heartbreak for me. Especially given my lack of experience. The sound of the engine became a purr. I was lost in Riggins' kisses. Until a light came on in windows behind us.

Riggins pulled away, smiling, his hair standing at odd angles from my passionate fondling.

"Is someone's dad onboard?" I laughed. "Is your captain watching out for your virtue?" I raised an eyebrow. "I've never seen this version of the old turn-on-the-porch-light trick."

The corners of Riggins' eyes crinkled adorably as he smiled. "I think the captain is trying to tell us, none too subtly, that it's time for dinner." He glanced at his watch. "Shit. I lost track of time. It *is* time for dinner. Late for dinner."

I'd been so lost in Riggins, every sense had been focused on him. As soon as he mentioned dinner, I smelled the delicious scent of something cooking. Right on cue, my stomach rumbled. I slid off his lap.

Riggins ran his fingers through his hair as I shook mine out. He signaled someone inside and offered me a hand up.

A waiter appeared, set a basket of bread on the table, and lit the candles. Riggins pulled a chair out for me. The waiter returned with salads and set them in front of us.

When the waiter left again, Riggins took my hand. "I have something I need to tell you."

CHAPTER SIX

*H*aley
Riggins looked suddenly serious. He had
that bad-news look on his face. I lost my
appetite, but managed to keep my fork from trembling
in my hand. "Yes?"

He seemed to hesitate. "It's been a fantastic day. It's
flown by. When I'm with you—"

He set his fork down with a bite of salad still on it. "I
didn't want to ruin the mood by talking business. But
all day I felt like I've been keeping something from
you."

I set my fork down now, too.

He took my hand. "You know, of course, that I took
Rose out last night." He paused. "She knows about the

will. Most of it she's guessed at. But she knows more than she should."

"What?" I went cold. I shouldn't have been surprised, but somehow I was. "How?"

He explained her methods. "She's made me an offer—if I choose her, she'll give me everything required for her share of the Dead Duke's mother's money. Then, if I want, or she and I want, she'll walk away amicably."

"Why didn't you tell me?" My voice shook. My mouth was dry.

He looked at me helplessly. "I was selfish. I wanted an unspoiled day with you. I wanted a repeat of our night of dancing together."

"Did you accept?" The words popped out. I was afraid of the answer.

He shook his head.

"But you're thinking about it?" I blinked, trying not to panic.

"I *have* to think about it."

"Because it's a business deal?" I took a deep breath to calm myself.

"Because it's an important decision with consequences for all of us." He took squeezed my hand. "Your fingers are cold."

My entire soul was ice.

"What do you want me to do? Do you want me to make the same offer? Match her terms? Beat them? I've already agreed to keep silent and help you find a way out. And abide by the terms if your out fails."

He shook his head. "No. Haley, please. Understand." He blew out a breath. "I'm giving you an out. If you want it. That's what today was partly about. I wanted you to get to know me better before I brought it up."

"You gave me a dream day." My heart raced. "Is that really you?"

"It's really me on a date." His expression was serious. "I wanted you to see the house and the boat. Where I went to school. To hear my dumb college stories. See how I live now. So you can decide if you still want to be a part of that. My lifestyle has its pros and cons."

I knew that only too well. I could already feel myself fading into the background. Riggins would always be the more popular face between the two of us. I didn't have the personality to become a real housewife. People would always want to know more about him than me.

And I was already being called a gold digger by some in the press. They didn't know our story. And I couldn't tell them the truth. It was a no-win scenario.

"You know her claims aren't verified?" I said. "Mr. Thorne is still trying to prove them. He thinks it could take longer than the time you have. Much longer than three weeks. Especially if I want it to."

Riggins nodded. "Yes. I know."

I took a deep breath. "He asked for my DNA. I haven't decided yet if I should give it to him. Is that what *you* want?"

He shook his head. "It's your decision. If you want out, this could be your ticket. Your DNA could definitively prove she's a descendant and related to you. But you also risk finding out she's mistaken."

That was putting it kindly.

"And lock yourself back into the role of reluctant duchess. If I can't find a way out for us then..."

The unsaid hung in the air.

"Does it matter what I want?" I stared at him. "You could always steal my DNA. Take it off any of the glasses I drank from today—"

He grabbed the water glass in front of me and hurled it over the side of the boat. His face was set and angry. Frustrated. "You'll have to trust me. I promise not to. You have my word."

I might have been a fool, but I believed him. "I'm not sure *what* I want."

Except that I wanted to be fair to everyone.

He nodded and let go of my hand. "That makes two of us."

"So Rose and I really *are* in a competition?"

He pursed his lips to one side. "It seems so. Unless a miracle occurs, I don't see a way out of this marriage, and the clock is ticking. That damn Dead Duke."

I lifted my chin and made a split-second decision, letting my heart talk. "I don't want out just yet. But I want you to have options. You have to know whether Rose is really a contender. My DNA could prove it one way or the other. Hang on."

Earlier in the day I had done something that not even Sid knew about. I'd bought a DNA kit. Just in case. And because I was conflicted. It was in my purse, which was on a nearby bench. I jumped up and got it before returning to my seat at the table.

I held the kit out. "See this?" I tore open the box. I'd read up on the instructions online. I pulled the swab out, ran it over the inside of my cheeks, and sealed it in the preaddressed, postage-paid envelope while Riggins sat in stunned silence.

I held the envelope out to him.

He didn't reach for it.

"There you go." I set it on the table between us. "Do with it what you want or feel you have to. The decision is totally yours. I already told you I'm not a materialistic person. I'm not sure I want to be duchess. Or a billionaire's wife. Certainly not if you prefer Rose over me. If you help Sid, that's all I need. But..."

He looked at me expectantly.

"I like you, Riggins. Really like you. I think...if circumstances were different...then, of course, we would never have met. Or, well, actually, we met, and I baked those mint brownies you love with extra care as I worshipped you from afar." I laughed nervously and glanced down. "But we probably would never have dated. What I'm trying to say is, even though you *are* a little old for me..."

He smiled at that.

"...I think we could have something special, given time. When I'm with you, I feel as comfortable as if I've known you forever. Like I can tell you everything and be honest. Like now.

"That's the true definition of a friend, at the very least. You can be apart for ages, but when you're together, it's like no time's passed and there's no awkwardness. Just that is a rare thing. But I feel a spark, too. It's just a little ember now."

He lifted an eyebrow and his Adam's apple bobbed.

"Okay, a white-*hot* ember. Who knows, though? The winds of life might blow it out.

"Or they might fan it like a bellows into a raging passion. An epic love. I'd like to know how that story plays out. Fate has dealt us a crap hand in the love game.

"I wish we had time to explore it before we made a major decision like getting married and agreeing to divorce. Neither one of us are ready for marriage now. So what I'm saying is this—if you aren't sure what you want yet, either, just keep me in the game. I'd like a shot at being your wife."

I could have been mistaken, but I thought his eyes misted over.

"Damn, Haley, you really know how to give a speech and make a point."

I nudged the envelope toward him. "Deal?"

He took it and held it up. "Deal."

"One condition?"

He nodded. "Yeah?"

"Don't tell me the results. If you choose Rose, I'll know anyway. If you choose me..." I shrugged. "I'd like to think it wasn't because you had to."

"*You* are amazing, Haley."

"Glad you think so." My heart was pounding loudly in my ears, drumming out a rhythm that told me I *might* have been amazing, but I was *definitely* stupid and reckless.

"Let's change the subject now!" I sounded too bright, even to my own ears. "Rose wants to see Wareswood Castle, the two of us. The late duchess grew up there. You should come along. Do a side-by-side comparison of Rose and me. See which of us looks better on your arm."

I laughed because there was nothing else I could do. "See if either of us look like any of those old, stuffy supposed ancestors of ours that I hear still hang in the place. Get used to the eyes of ancestors following you around."

"You want me tagging along on your girls' day out?" He looked surprised, but pleased.

"Why not?" I said as breezily as I could. "The media will have a field day. Though it might be bad news for American/British relations. Still, I think it would be a good show. We can post pictures on social media and increase the speculation."

Riggins relaxed and grinned full-out. "Okay, then. It's a date." He paused. "I have an idea."

"Yeah?"

"Why don't we make a party out of it? A real spectacle. Spend the whole weekend there. Rent the entire place out and have the run of it."

"Hmmm..." I said. "That *would* give us a decent shot at running into Helen's mother's ghost. Which Rose was quite excited about."

Riggins laughed. "Not sure about the ghost. We can certainly invite her. The main thing is, we can get to know each other. Bring your sister. I'll invite some friends. I'll see about renting it out."

"It will be almost like our own little version of *The Bachelor*. Let the duchess contest begin." I tried to sound brighter than I felt.

His smile was tentative. "There's one more thing." He reached out and squeezed my hand. "I'm not a eunuch or as gentlemanly as I seem." He told me about the pregnancy clause of the will.

"So we're not taking any chances?" I wasn't sure if I was relieved or not. It took the pressure off me. But when my secret was revealed?

"Sadly, no."

"There go my fantasies of doing it on a yacht." I tugged his hand playfully.

"Believe me, I've thought about it." His eyes were dark and wide. "I've thought about a lot of things. Like taking you back to one of the bedrooms onboard and doing everything but." His voice was low and sexy, intimate.

My toes curled at the thought of being with him. I clenched my legs together. My breathing became shallow.

"There's just too damn much at stake here to take any chances." He sounded genuinely regretful.

We were still holding hands. He squeezed mine.

"You could always get us both pregnant. That would get you out of the marriage."

"I'm not that big of an asshole." His gaze held mine. "Besides, it would only delay the inevitable for nine months."

"Forty weeks, if you want to be completely accurate," I said.

CHAPTER SEVEN

*R*iggins
   If time would only trickle slowly when I was with Haley, instead of flying by. All too soon, we docked. I held Haley's hand as we walked on the dock and up the lawn toward the house.

   "It must still be early," I said without looking at my watch. I knew from the position of the stars that it wasn't. But what the hell? "Want to watch a movie in my theater?"

   She paused, pretending to think about it. "Is that just an excuse to sit side by side and fondle my breasts? Maybe neck?"

   "Absolutely."

   She laughed. "Well..."

"I'll fire up the popcorn machine. I'll even throw in real butter."

"Tempting offer. What kind of movie did you have in mind? Romantic comedy? Chick flick? Or guy-type action adventure?"

"Whatever you want to see." I let us into the house.

"Good answer." She laughed, evilly and teasingly.

"What?"

"I wouldn't mind watching another one of those shows about famous estates and how dukes really live."

"Why?" I turned to face her. "I believe you."

"Yeah, but I really think you should see them."

"You just want to watch my reaction to them."

She laughed outright. "Yeah. You're right. Still game?"

I pulled her into a kiss. "You're such a brat."

And so we watched a documentary about one of Britain's most famous estates and the duke and duchess who ran it. Haley picked seats in the center of the theater in the middle row of five.

"So you're one of those. Someone who likes to be right in the middle," I teased as I took a seat next to her and put the armrest between us up.

"To be honest, choosing a seat in a private theater where we're the only guests for the show is completely new to me. Middle seemed logical." Her grin was impish and completely sexy. "In a normal theater, I prefer the center of the first row behind the handicap seats so I can put my foot on the rail. And because those seats are rarely used, so there's little chance of anyone obstructing my view."

"Good logic," I said.

She kicked off her shoes and curled her legs beneath her in the seat. I was too large for that and in awe of her ability to fit into it like that.

"Popcorn?" she said.

I turned the machine on. Then pulled up the menu and scrolled through until I found the show she wanted.

"I haven't seen that one."

I got us a bucket of popcorn and sat next to her with the popcorn between so we could share.

"You're a billionaire and you didn't get me my own bucket of popcorn from the machine you own? What a cheapskate!"

"Sharing's nicer." I bumped her with my shoulder.

She laughed. "I see your plan. Since we're on a no-sex, no-temptation plan, you're just hoping for a little accidental finger-brushing action."

"Curses! Foiled again. You saw right through me."

She pursed her lips comically. I kissed them. She was so damn cute and irresistible.

She laughed. "Play the movie."

I started the show. I settled in with one arm around her, nice and gentlemanly, and the other on the popcorn bucket, intentionally brushing her fingers with mine and going for the same kernels. She laughed and slapped my hand away.

So I slid my hand down off her shoulder and cupped her breast.

"Hey!" She shook her head.

"Don't like it?" I sure as hell did.

She grinned and crunched her popcorn. "I'd be disappointed if you didn't grope me."

She made me feel young and normal. Down to earth.

"Oh, look! Here comes the duke. Pay attention. You could learn a thing or two from him. This is you now. Your life."

I sighed and shook my head as we watched the duke talk about preserving the family art and saving costs while heating and renovating a dusty castle.

"Did you ever think," she said, "that he's your peer?" She laughed. "Like your *literal* peer. That's probably where the term 'peer' comes from. He's a peer and your peer—"

"Do you always talk through shows?" I gave her a squeeze.

"Only in home theaters."

"Lucky me."

"He could end up being one of your best friends, too. I mean, you might end up sitting next to him in the House of Lords or at tea with the Queen."

"Stop."

She laughed again.

The duke put on a pair of rubber boots and went out to talk to his gamekeeper about not letting the deer population on the property get out of hand and to inspect a muddy road.

Haley nudged me. "Are you observing dukely fashion?"

"He's wearing rubber boots."

"No. He's wearing wellies. You need to get up to date with your British. Maybe you should even study it.

Take a foreign language course—British for American Dummies." She laughed.

I rolled my eyes and laughed. "Maybe you should, too."

She shook her head. "No thanks. I'm already better at British than you are."

"Really?"

"I knew what wellies are."

"Astound me with something else."

She shrugged. "What do the British mean when they say 'self-drive car'?"

"Those haven't been invented yet, have they? Though we're close. We have cars that can park for you."

"They mean rental car." She sighed in mock exasperation. "What's a tip and run?"

"Is that anything like a dine and dash?"

She shook her head. "It's a hit and run."

"Probably by that self-drive car," I said. "You've been studying."

"Maybe. I like to know what I might be getting into." She paused. "But it's not like *I* have to. I'm just in the running for the ancillary role of duchess. I can be totally American and get away with it. The American heiresses of Helen's generation made it vogue."

She pointed to the screen. "You'd look so completely adorable in wellies. And one of those natty hunting suits. I wonder if your gamekeeper wears one like that? With the hat."

I shook my head again and laughed. I hadn't felt so light and carefree in years.

After the show ended, we sat and talked.

"One thing that sucks about being a billionaire?" she asked.

I had to think about it a minute. "Gifts."

"What?" She tilted her head. "You're the man who's impossible to buy for? No one else can match what you can buy for yourself. Wait. Don't you have billionaire friends? Surely they can come up with some nice crap."

"No." I shook my head. "I mean buying gifts for other people. I grew up without money. I come from the middle class. I know what that life's like. And how money influences everything.

"Now I have plenty. I can buy what I want. Most things that are expensive to other people seem cheap to me. It's easy to scare people away with gifts that are too expensive." I was testing her out. Seeing what her opinion on expensive gifts was.

"You mean like buckets of popcorn?" She grinned impishly.

I laughed. "I mean like a hundred-dollar scarf or a five-hundred-dollar purse."

"Oh!" She nodded. "We're talking about women here. That's where the frightening gifts come from. Are most of the women you date not from money, then?"

"A few." I stared at her.

She pursed her lips, considering it. "I can see your point. Expensive gifts *can* make the non-gold-digging, non-user type of person feel uncomfortable. Especially when you can't reciprocate in kind. And they can make you feel obligated to the other person, too."

I smiled. I liked her answer. It was completely in character for her. She wasn't the gold-digging kind of girl.

"Would you like to see the ring?" I said on impulse. I didn't know why it mattered, but I wanted her opinion on it. "Helen's ring. The one the Dead Duke has mandated I propose with."

"Oh!" She nodded. "Is that what Mr. Thorne handed you at the meeting?"

"Yeah. It must have had sentimental value for the old codger, the Dead Duke."

She bit her lip and took a deep breath. "I wondered. I've been curious about it. I *love* antique jewelry. I just haven't been able to afford any. Is it nice?"

"That's a matter of opinion. Apparently it comes with the job." I paused. "Look. Women are particular about their engagement rings. The woman I marry is entitled to pick out her own. If the new duchess wants something different, she can just drag out the old ring for ceremonial occasions."

"Like running the tourist shop?"

"Exactly that." I grinned at her. "So? Want to see it?"

"Yeah. Sure. *Obviously.* I'm dying of curiosity now."

"Hang on. I'll be right back." I retrieved it from my office.

When I returned, she was sitting, feet curled up in the theater seat, finishing the last of the popcorn while she waited for me. My heart pounded as I opened the box and held it out to her. For some damn reason, I wanted to please her.

She took the box tentatively and studied it. Her eyes went wide. "Art deco." She sounded almost reverent. "I love that period. That's what I was guessing. If Helen got it new. But then, I thought, maybe the ring had been the Dead Duke's mother's or something."

"Hers went down with the *Titanic*, I think."

"Oh." Haley blinked. "How tragic." She took a closer look at the ring. "All diamonds. No sapphires or emeralds."

"Is that disappointing?"

"No. It's stunning. It's just that in that period, many engagement rings had other precious stones. I love sapphires, and real emeralds, not lab-created ones, are rare. But this is truly beautiful. How many carats would you guess? The large diamond in the center looks to me to be about three."

I nodded. "That looks about right."

"White gold or platinum?"

"Platinum."

"Well." She handed it back. "It's gorgeous. Large. Certainly expensive. Hard to tell exactly *how* expensive without knowing the quality of the diamonds. They look flawless to the naked eye, at least. Whoever selected it—Helen or the Dead Duke—had good taste. Looking at it makes me wonder about them. Makes them real, don't you think?"

I shrugged. "I hadn't thought about it."

She took another look at the ring. "It's in immaculate condition. But then, the duchess died young. She wouldn't have had it long, and it's obviously been recently cleaned and polished to its original brilliance.

"The Dead Duke would have been on the impover-ished side, for him, anyway, when he gave it to Helen. That would have been before he used his financial ge-nius to increase the small amount of money his mother left him. He was marrying Helen to save the dukedom." She glanced at me and laughed. "For her money, in his case.

"Do you think this ring says he loved her?"

"I don't know," I said, honestly.

"Hmmm." She seemed mesmerized by it. "Or only that he wanted to impress her? Or it was a matter of pride to show off? Did he spend more for it than he could comfortably afford at the time? Take her tastes into consideration?

"I've seen art deco period rings with about as many carats on Etsy for around thirty grand. Enough for someone to kosh your duchess over the head for it. Ceremonial occasions only, I'd say."

I was happy she liked it. Way happier than I should have been. I hated to tell her, but if her estimate was right, that would be the cheapest piece of jewelry my duchess would own, as a matter of pride. And I was willing to spend a boatload more on a woman I loved.

Haley

At four a.m. I tried to sneak back into my house without waking anyone. Sid popped right up and met me in the hall, turning on the light and startling me.

She wore a disappointed expression and had her hands on her hips. "What are *you* doing home so early?

I was hoping you'd spend the night with him." She sounded like a scolding mother.

I laughed. "It's that horrible pregnancy clause."

She frowned, puzzled and sleepy-eyed. "I must not be awake enough. I don't understand. Pregnancy clause?"

I explained.

"But you're on birth control," she said.

I was. For my painful periods, among other things.

"Birth control isn't one hundred percent effective. We can't take *any* chances." I laughed.

She looked skeptical. "He doesn't have sexual problems, does he?"

"No," I said. "Trust me."

She shrugged. "But it went all right?"

"It went perfectly!" I didn't tell her about giving him my DNA. It was a good thing I couldn't stop beaming.

She studied me then broke into a sleepy smile. "Good! I can see that. I want to hear all about it."

"In the morning."

"It is the morning."

"I meant after we get some sleep," I said. "After I get some and you get more."

The next morning, Sid was up before I was. She was sitting at the table, reading something on her phone. She got up and poured me a cup of coffee and slid her phone over for me to see.

"What's this?"

"An article I found by a woman who dated a billionaire for a while and what she learned. Read it."

"Before I've had my coffee?"

She set a cup in front of me. "I want you to be prepared for what you're getting into."

I sighed and read aloud. "'Number one—billionaires have great PR people. Before I started dating the billionaire, I Googled him. His press was great. Turns out he wasn't. His press said he was a warm, kind, humble philanthropist. He was a full-of-himself cheapskate.'" I glanced at Sid. "Riggins is a nice person. And not stingy. Except with his popcorn."

Sid didn't get the inside joke.

"Tons of success and billions of dollars will give anyone an ego."

Sid sat down next to me.

"Riggins is just a regular guy," I reassured her. "'You'll always live in his shadow,'" I read. "Okay, that one might have some merit. The press will always be about him.

"'And lastly, no matter what you do or what you think, or how many gifts you turn down or accept, people will always accuse you of being a gold digger.'" I nodded. "So true." I slid Sid's phone to her.

"You're not scared off?"

I shook my head. "Not at all. Riggins is different. But it's sweet of you to care. Hey!" I said. "He's invited you to come with us and spend the weekend at Wareswood Castle. We're going to have a combination house party and duchess contest."

Riggins

If I had been concerned about losing my heart before, spending the day with Haley reaffirmed it. I liked being with her. Too much. There was something genuine and fresh about her. She wasn't pretentious. And she was so damn loyal to her sister and those she loved. She was even loyal to me. Not that I deserved it, necessarily. I was still out for number one.

But what other woman would have handed me her DNA with such bravado and effectively given me a way to cut her out of several hundred million dollars? Her sense of right and fairness was admirable, if naive. She seemed so damn unimpressed by my wealth. And more interested in me.

I wasn't insensible to how rare that was. Especially in a woman as young as she was. It took incredible confidence in herself. And confidence was always sexy.

But now I wondered what I would do. Did I choose the lady or the tiger? And who was who?

I dropped the DNA test in the mail and called Thorne to ask him to get Rose's for comparison.

On Monday, I drove the Lamborghini to work. I pulled into the parking garage and squealed around the corners. When I got to my reserved spot, someone had a hung a new sign.

Duke Parking Only

The aristocratic kind

Below it was a mock Feldhem family crest—a felt ham in a shield with two crossed swords.

Damn that Justin! This could only be his work. I made a mental note to get him back.

To my pleasant surprise, the parking garage was quiet. I jumped out of the car and took the sky bridge across to the office. Even though we had grown tremendously in the last couple of years, Flash retained the feeling of a small firm that was like family. I didn't have a private entrance or a private elevator. Neither Jus nor I did. We walked the floors and chatted with our employees. Played Ping-Pong on break. Had an open-door policy. It was one of the things that made Flash so great.

I took the elevator from the second-floor sky bridge level to the ground floor to go in through badge check. When the elevator doors pinged open, the peace and quiet was shattered by a mob of women wearing the duke's personal fan club T-shirts in navy blue with the Union Jack, holding banners that said "Dukes Do It With Style," and screaming.

"There he is! That's him!"

I reached for the button to close the doors too late. One of my fans got her foot in and stopped the door from closing. I was barraged with a volley of flying panties being snapped at me like rubber bands. Damn, they had some fine elastic. One woman swooned and passed out.

Another threw herself at me and wrapped her arms around my neck. A third held out a pen and asked me to sign her breast.

A camera crew was catching it all on film for the noon news.

Fortunately, my security team stepped in, pried the woman off me, dispatched the woman offering her breast, surrounded me, and escorted me through the throng. My receptionist looked harried as we passed her. She was surrounded by extra security, too.

The team got me past the badge check and into the secure confines of the offices.

I thanked the team and spent a minute strategizing with them about how to handle the disturbance before heading to my office, trailing thong panties as I went.

Jus was waiting for me in my office, sitting in a chair, working on his laptop. He grinned when I walked in. "Good morning, Your Grace. Forgive me if I don't stand and bow."

"Felt ham, really? Duke parking only?" I raised an eyebrow.

He laughed. "Are you modeling a new line of panties for one of our events?" He pointed to my shoulder and hair. "Interesting way to showcase them."

"Shit." I picked a pink thong off my shoulder, snapped it at him, and dusted a blue lace number out of my hair.

"Not entranced with your fans, duke?"

I scowled at him and closed the door. "Any luck over the weekend?"

"Nothing. Nada. Zip. That Dead Duke of yours was smarter than we originally gave him credit for. I've tried hacking into his computers. They're locked up tight. Not even my friend Dex could get in or find any-thing. But it looks like that might be moot now, with you having another choice."

"Yeah. But I need to know if she's legit." And whether I should mail Haley's DNA to the lab. "What are you and Kayla doing this weekend? I'm planning a house party at Wareswood Castle and I'd like you to come."

Jus frowned. "A house party? What the hell is that?"

"I'm renting the entire place out. Haley and her sister will be there. Lady Rose. Myself."

"Oh. I get it. You're offering us a front-row seat while you choose your duchess. How could I turn that down? I'll have to check with the boss, of course. But it sounds like the kind of entertainment she'll enjoy."

"Great! I need her help."

"You're going to put my pregnant wife to work?" He looked surprised and curious.

"In a manner of speaking. I need her to make a point of how uncomfortable and hard pregnancy is."

Justin raised an eyebrow. "I see where you're going with this. Kay doesn't exactly love being pregnant like some women. And she's ready to be done. She's not exactly hating it, either. But she could come up with something. Trying to scare off one of the contenders with fears of pregnancy?"

"Astute." I nodded and grinned. "What about Lazer? Think he'd enjoy it?"

Jus shot me a surprised look and snickered. "You must be desperate. You and Lazer don't typically get along."

"Our competition is all in good fun," I said. "I think in this case, he may come in very handy. He has skills, and a title—Northwest's Hottest Bachelor—that I need."

"Now you're just dangling temptation in front of the potential duchesses, aren't you?" Jus said.

I grinned. "Think Lazer will protest? Hitting on two hot women is rough duty. If he's not man enough for the job—"

"You're playing with fire," Jus said. "What if he peels them both off? He *is* the hottest bachelor."

I laughed. "I'm more afraid he won't detach either of them."

Jus shook his head. "Given what you have in mind, I don't see how Lazer could resist. Make sure you fill him in."

Jus and I discussed a few more issues, mostly Flash business. He was just leaving when there was a knock on the door.

Jennifer stepped in with a package in her hand. "This just arrived for you, Riggins."

"Is it from one of my fans downstairs in the lobby?" I eyed it cautiously.

"I don't think so, boss. It's from that big major online retailer who shall not be named. The one whose headquarters are just a few blocks away from us. The one who likes to compete with us where our product lines overlap with theirs, poach our employees, and whose goal is to take over the world." She was grinning. "It was delivered by a major carrier. Same-day service."

We were always joking about them. Flash's early years of growth had outpaced theirs. I can't tell you how happy that made me.

"A fan could have ordered it," I said, grumpily.

Jus stopped in the doorway next to Jennifer. "Maybe it's another thong. Do you have a green one yet?"

"Shut up." I glared at him.

"Should I call security? Have them check it out for bombs and dangerous lingerie?" Justin winked at Jennifer.

"It feels like a book, boss. That *is* their specialty."

"Maybe it's a book of love poetry. An ode to a duke," Jus said very helpfully as he took the package from Jennifer and held it out to me. "Open it! Open it! Your safety is my first concern. I'm not leaving until you do."

I snatched the book from him, pulled the strip tab to open it, and slid a paperback book out. "*The British to American English Compendium?*"

I smiled. Damn, I couldn't help it. A gift receipt was stuck to the front.

Time to get your British on, Duke. Cake and ale are over. I'm certainly not one to make a long nose at the opportunity before me. I'll be bringing my A-game to our next amusement. And no, I don't mean carnival ride.

Looking forward to the weekend!

Haley

PS If you don't understand this message, use the book.

I broke out laughing. Haley had just sent me the perfect gift. Damn.

Justin stared at me. "Who's it from?"

"Haley."

"Smart girl," he said. "One point for her. Now that the danger's passed, I'm out of here."

"Inside joke," I said to Jennifer. How did you say that in British?

CHAPTER EIGHT

Haley

On Monday, I was nervous. What would Riggins think of the gift I'd sent him? It was meant to be flirty and fun. Intimate. And to show, of course, that I wasn't cheap. What do you give the guy who has everything? The gift of laughter, of course. With a dose of foreign language thrown in for good measure. Haha.

I was on pins and needles as I waited for a response. I'd sent it with same-day delivery, but there was no telling when, exactly, it would arrive. Actually, I was just hoping *for* a response and that Riggins wasn't totally distracted by the arrival of his panty-throwing fan club. Guys, you tell me—was it really titillating to have sexy panties tossed at you? Were you supposed to im-

agine that the panty thrower was now commando and
waiting for you?

I'd never actually heard of the opposite—guys
throwing their boxers and tighty whities at hot women.
Not that I'd heard of everything. I was pretty naïve
when it came down to it. I supposed that if some guy
ever threw his underwear at me I would just be hoping
they were clean. Now, on second thought, I wondered if
I should have sent Riggins a thong panty in the old red,
white, and blue along with that compendium? Tactical
mistake?

His plane full of British groupies mobbing him was
all over the news and social media. There was one completely hilarious picture of Riggins putting up his arms
to shield himself from a volley of panty fire that was
trending everywhere. I was wondering just how he
planned to ditch his admiring horde in the long run. If
they showed up at the castle, that could be awkward.

Finally, my phone buzzed with a text from Riggins.
My heart pounded in my ears as I read it.

*After a bad patch this morning, I spoke with the
bailiff of the castle and booked the weekend. He as-
sured me the bedmakers won't even be seen and the
period bedside lockers are both functional and beautiful.*

*I hope this isn't a balls-up. I spent a fair amount of
bean on this party. But why do it on a bootlace when I
can afford more? Bad form to mention that?*

*I'm chuffed about this weekend and eager to see you
again.*

I laughed aloud when I read it. My thumbs flew as I texted back.

Haha. You're just stuck in the B's of that book I sent you. You're going to need more than that to be fluent in British, Duke.

PS I'm looking forward to the weekend, too. Should I bring extra panties to toss at you? I hear that's a thing now.

Thought bubbles came on my screen while he texted back.

What does a guy have to do to impress you? I just got this book a few minutes ago. Getting to the B's already is moving lightning fast. Did you notice I even threw in a C-word? BTW, thank you. This book is great and makes me laugh.

PS Please, no more panty throwing. I may be scarred for life from this experience. I like to be the one removing the panties, not the one being pelted with them.

I couldn't stop smiling. Top that, Lady Rose!

On Tuesday, Riggins sent Sid and me an engraved invitation to Wareswood Castle. It was hand-delivered by courier. Sid and I decided getting a formal invitation was the height of classiness. A text or an email would have sufficed. But now we had a memento of the event for our scrapbooks.

I had the feeling going old school was part of the theme of the weekend, a step back in time. And something of an inside joke. We RSVPed immediately, both of us impressed at the pull Riggins had with a printer, and the castle, to get this put together in less than two days. We also had the feeling we'd be impressed with the guest list. We'd find out soon enough.

On Tuesday morning, the bakery was packed with British tourists, mostly Riggins' fan club, trying to get a look at the American competition—me. Makeup-less and hair in a net, I hid in the back. I mean, really! I shouldn't have to worry about putting makeup on at two in the morning. I could barely wake up.

On Tuesday afternoon, the news story broke that Lady Rose had toured Flashionista's offices and met key staff, including Riggins' partner, Justin Green. A good time was had by all. At least if the pictures were any indication.

Crap. Now she had a leg up on me.

The gossip rags had already picked up on the fact that Riggins had been seen in the company of two women recently—Lady Rose and me. Speculation flew. Was history repeating itself? Was love echoing through time? Would one of the late Seattle heiress Helen Feldhem's descendants be the next Duchess of Witham?

The city was pulling for me, their native daughter. Radio stations started call-in polls. Online polls sprang everywhere.

In early results, I was winning, by the way. But then, the population of the US was much greater than the UK's. So maybe it wasn't a fair fight, even if they did have Canada and Australia. The media focus was so intense I worried that the truth would somehow get out. I also wondered if Riggins had sent that DNA sample in.

Reporters began trailing me and begging for interviews in even greater force. My social media accounts
exploded, bombarded with friend requests and private
messages. Curious crowds mobbed the bakery. And
Seattle boutiques offered to lend me clothes, even give
them to me, if I would parade around in them and "just
casually mention" where I got them. In other words,
promote them and lead the public to believe I was part
of their clientele. I turned them down. I didn't want to
owe anyone anything.

The situation was overwhelming. I had a hard time
working and concentrating.

That night, Riggins called me. "How are you holding up? I see you're ahead in the entertainment polls.
The Duchess Contest." He laughed. "It has a nice ring
to it."

"Nice of you to notice." I laughed, but it was embar-
rassing. Not the way I'd planned to live my life.

"I'm up by ten points in aggregate. Even allowing
for margin of error, my campaign manager and social
media savant—Sid—feels confident we can maintain
our lead. Barring any major hit piece, of course. If this
were a presidential election, I'd win in a landslide."

A competition for his heart was another matter altogether.

"People are voting straight down patriotic lines. My
constituency is much larger than hers. It's a slam dunk
for me. With the public, anyway."

I charged ahead, not wanting him to think I was
hinting for something. "How goes it in the world of
panty tossing? Must be hideous being mobbed by ador-

ing women all the time and having panties raining around you like confetti."

I could almost hear his scowl.

He actually growled, deep in his throat. The sound was so hot I had to clench my legs.

"Yeah, delightful." He paused. "I'm sorry I got you into this."

"It's not your fault. I blame the Dead Duke and my unfortunate ancestry. You're off the hook, Living Duke. How's your studying going? Getting any better at British?"

"I could use some quizzing."

I tested him on a few British phrases. "Expect a pop quiz from time to time to keep you on your toes."

He laughed. "As they say, 'Two great nations separated by a common language.'"

I laughed, too.

"You're a nice bit of crumpet, Haley," he said in a lecherous voice. "I can hardly wait for the weekend."

"Did you just compliment me and call me attractive in British?"

"Two points for you. But I really am looking forward to seeing you again."

My heart raced. Neither of us brought up the DNA test.

"What are you doing tomorrow morning?" Riggins asked, almost too casually.

My hopes soared. "I get off work early tomorrow. I'm just going in to bake and will be out before they open at six thirty. The Blackberry has been cutting my hours. At least until the curiosity wears off or I lose the duchess competition, I'm not allowed during open hours. My presence is creating too much of a distraction."

He paused. "Will you be home by ten?"

"Should be."

"Good! I have a surprise for you." He sounded pleased with himself. "A special delivery."

"Is it a pony?" I smiled. "I've always wanted one."

"No." His sexy voice had a smile in it. "You'll have to wait and see."

On Wednesday morning after work, Sid and I were debating what to pack for the weekend. And trying to pretend we weren't excited about my surprise and eyeing the clock every three seconds, eager for ten o'clock to come.

As usual, I had nothing in my closet that Sid deemed appropriate for such a momentous event, except the dress I'd gotten during my spa day at the spy school. And Riggins had already seen it and my photo had already been splashed all over the Internet in it. I was insisting that jeans and cute tops should be good enough when the doorbell rang.

"Our delivery!" we said in unison, and headed for the door.

Sid got there first. In just a few short days, we'd learned not to just throw the door open. To check first. We'd had a few weirdoes stop by, and the media was always trying to snap a picture of us.

Sid looked through the keyhole. "It's our delivery!" She threw open the door.

Two young women stood on our stoop. I recognized them from the bakery. They were Flashionista girls, regulars at the Blackberry. A Flashionista van was parked in our driveway.

The taller of the two spoke. "Haley Hamilton?"

I nodded. "I'm Haley and this is my sister Sid."

The shorter girl smiled. "We'd recognize you anywhere, but we had to ask. I'm Erica and this is Paige. We're here to outfit you for your weekend at the castle, courtesy of Riggins and Flashionista! We were handpicked for the job by the head buyer, Marla. Riggins said to tell you he wanted the playing field level. And the American candidate to be clothed by Flash."

"But we can't accept—" I started.

"Oh, yes we can!" Sid said. She whispered to me, "We can at least see what they brought. We'd be helping Riggins out. Promo for Flash."

Erica clapped. "Excellent! This is going to be fun. We have a bunch of stuff in the van." She eyed the surroundings. "Can we bring it in through the garage? Fewer steps, I'm guessing?"

Sid pushed in front of me. "That would be perfect! Can we help?"

"I think it's safer if you stay inside." Paige nervously eyed the sidewalk, where a crowd of tourists and paparazzi gathered. "We'll get one of the security guys to help us if we need it."

It was getting ridiculous. Riggins had sent over a security team to keep the curious off the grass and away from us.

"Just open the garage door and relax," Paige said.

The two of them trotted off while Sid opened the garage door for them. And I watched them open the back of the van, slide out a ramp, and roll a rack full of clothes out the back of the van.

It took the Flash girls and two security guys three loads to haul everything in—two wheeling racks of clothes and over six boxes of shoes, jewelry, and accessories. Sid's eyes went wide at the sight. Tired as she was, she bounced around, going through the racks, drooling over the clothes.

Erica studied us and nodded to Paige. "I think we got their sizes about right." She guided Sid to one rack. "This is yours. I studied your online profiles to determine your style. I think I got it right. I hope so! I hope you like what I've brought.

"Riggins told us to bring evening wear, garden party clothes, casual clothes, even nighties and robes. We brought it all!"

I turned to Erica. "You were in charge of my wardrobe, then, I take it?"

She grinned. "Same MO." She pointed me toward the rack. "We've been instructed to put together outfits for specific occasions. And then throw a few extra choices in for good measure." She pulled the lid off a box full of beautiful costume jewelry packed individually in plastic bags. "What do you want to try on first?"

Sid was already digging in, chatting happily with Paige, and becoming fast friends. They spoke the same language—fashion. She was telling Paige how she'd love to work at Flash after she graduated.

If she graduates. If her health allows, I thought, remembering why I was doing all this. My heart was bursting at seeing her so animated and happy. I felt uncomfortable and overwhelmed by the expensive clothes. But if this made Sid happy, we could at least try a few things on. Maybe keep a *few*.

Erica and I got off to a slower start.

"I recognize you from the bakery. You come in a lot," I said, trying to make conversation.

"I do! I love the Blackberry, especially their currant scones. Are you responsible for those? If so, I hate you!" She laughed. "I've put on five pounds because of them. Think you can sneak me out the recipe?" She winked.

I liked her.

Four hours, a delicious delivered lunch, compliments of Riggins, and endless clothing changes later, Sid and I each had a new wardrobe of clothes. More than enough for a weekend. More like enough for a month-long vacation.

Erica and Paige laid them out across our living room, snapping photos of what went with what and texting them to me.

"We can't take all this!" I said as Paige called a security guy to help her wheel out the discarded options. "It's too much. They're too expensive."

I was already in enough debt to Riggins and uncomfortable about the spa day with Milia. I couldn't keep taking things from him.

Sid stood quietly by, but I could see how much she wanted everything.

Paige waved her hand, brushing me off. "Riggins said you'd say that."

"I only want what we can afford." I sighed, knowing how disappointed Sid would be. Because we could afford maybe one thing apiece.

Paige turned to Erica. "He called that right, too."

"Here's the deal," Erica said to me. "All of this, everything we brought, are samples from our sample closet. Vendors send them to us. And then don't want them back. It's cheaper for us to just keep them after we're done with them than ship them back.

"Flash usually sells them at their monthly sample sales for pennies on the dollar and donates all the proceeds from the sample sale to the children's hospital. Riggins and Justin always make huge donations to the hospital in addition."

Paige nodded.

"Riggins gave us complete authority. He said that if you insisted on paying, we were to play—what did he call it?" She turned to Paige.

"Shop assistant," Paige said.

I grinned. Riggins wouldn't stop with the British. "Clerk."

Erica nodded. "Yes, like the clerks at the sample sale. They have complete discretion in how much to charge. So, if you insist on paying, twenty dollars ought to do it. We'll throw it into the fund for the hospital at the next sample sale for you and we're good."

"Twenty apiece," I said. I had that much in my purse.

Erica looked to Paige. Paige nodded.

"Sold!" Erica grinned.

I handed her two twenties. She tucked them in her pocket and signaled to one of the security guys. He brought four suitcases in from the van.

"These are included in the price," Erica said. "One last caveat—if asked, please mention you're wearing clothes you bought from Flash?"

I laughed and nodded. Riggins was exploiting every angle, I'd give him that. But he had me where he wanted me. I'd help him any way I could.

Erica and Paige leaned together toward me.

Paige whispered, "We hope you win! We both voted for you!"

CHAPTER NINE

*R*iggins
Rose called me. "Of course I accept your invitation, Riggins. I'm absolutely thrilled. Did Haley tell you about our plans to tour the castle?" Although her tone was breezy, there was an edge of jealousy to it, an edge I recognized all too well.

"Possibly."

Rose laughed delicately. "Have you thought about my offer?"

"I'm still considering it." I didn't like having the screws applied. "It's not a limited-time offer, is it?"

"No, of course. Absolutely not. I'm simply impatient, Riggins. We'd be such a *beautiful* arranged couple. And, even though the offer on my part has no limit, time is of the essence and running out quickly, as you well know. Although the wedding will certainly have to be an elopement at this late date, a future duchess would still like a bit of time to find a suitable dress.

"Are you still concerned with my authenticity?" She almost sounded pouty. "I gave Mr. Thorne my DNA sample. Right in front of his eyes. I heard my distant cousin gave hers, too. And Mr. Thorne expedited the tests. You'll see soon enough that I'm exactly who I say I am—your perfect duchess."

"I hope so," I said. "Impress me this weekend." While I spoke about being impressed, I was thinking of Haley.

"So that's it, is it? Haley and I are in direct competition for the title this weekend." She paused. When she spoke again, her voice was full of seduction. "Do you promise to propose at the end of the weekend?"

Haley

On Saturday afternoon at two, Riggins sent a car to take Sid and me to the castle. It was nearly February, and January was going out with a burst of winter. The day was bright and sunny, but cold. For Seattle, anyway. High thirties. The morning had been foggy. The fog had burned off, for the most part, but still hung in pockets here and there. The weather report was warning of nighttime freezing fog and frost. The frost wouldn't be any more brittle than my nerves. And the fog would provide a nice, creepy atmosphere to go ghost hunting. Or husband hunting, as the case may be.

The driver crammed our new sets of luggage stuffed with our Flashionista wardrobes in, and we were off. Wareswood Castle was just south of Seattle on its own private lake about an hour away. We were staying for exactly one night, but we had enough changes of clothes for twenty.

The drive through traffic to the castle was uneventful. Sid was uncharacteristically quiet. We both knew the stakes. I had an important decision to make, one that had as much to do with my heart as anything. We pulled onto a private road and wound through woods and gardens, past silent, giant Douglas firs, dogwoods still bare and without buds, and rhododendrons dormant for winter. In just another month or two, the gardens and grounds would burst into spring bloom and be gorgeous. Too bad the Dead Duke hadn't lived a bit longer.

"This is how the drive to Witham House will be," Sid whispered. "Past impressive grounds."

I nodded, lost in my thoughts and nerves. Sid and I had talked ourselves out. Nothing remained but to watch things unfold.

The castle loomed large and impressive at the end of a circular drive.

"Wow." Sid took it in. "It looks more like a Jane Eyre kind of castle than something from a fairytale."

"It's Tudor Gothic." I texted Riggins that we'd arrived. "It's *supposed* to be imposing."

My stomach was full of butterflies. Everything hinged on this weekend. Yes, Riggins would still help Sid. But I could be sure and do so much more if I were in the driver's seat as his wife. And then there was my heart to think about. As much as I wanted to deny it, it was hopelessly lost to him. I was in love, or, at least, falling in love with Riggins. The way it looked now, no other guy would ever measure up. I either lost him or made memories for a lifetime this weekend.

A car pulled in behind us. Another of Riggins' guests, I assumed.

Riggins was waiting for us on the circular drive when we pulled up, along with a bellman dressed like a footman of old in a coat and tails. The footman opened the door and handed us out of the car as a gorgeous white luxury car pulled up behind us. I was no good with cars so I couldn't say what the make and model were, only that it looked expensive.

As always when I caught a glimpse of Riggins, my heart fluttered wildly. He was dressed in jeans and a sweater and stood casually, hands in pockets. How was it that he always looked so hot? He'd made my heart race since the first time he'd come into the bakery. It sounded corny, but my breath caught. I wanted him. I wanted that man. Just looking at him made me smile.

He waved and walked toward us as the footman loaded our luggage on a cart and the driver got out of the car behind us. Riggins hugged me and Sid in turn. And gave instructions to the footman, just like a real duke. "Take their luggage to the Pink Poppy room. I've put them in the adjoining suites."

The footman nodded and wheeled off just as the driver of the white car called out to us. "Riggins, old bean!"

Riggins set his jaw, shook his head, and laughed as the newcomer clapped him on the back. "Lazer. Since when do you have a Bentley Mulsanne?"

Ah. So that's what the car was.

"Like it?" Lazer's voice was smooth and confident. "I bought it just for the weekend, Duke." He winked at Sid and me. "A British car seemed appropriate for a British weekend."

"You're not casting your vote for a British duchess, though, I hope?" I couldn't believe I'd spoken. And blatantly referenced what was at stake. Though everyone knew it. It had been all over the news. Or that my voice came out just the tiniest bit flirty.

Lazer's grin deepened. "I didn't realize my choice of car could be misconstrued as my vote. I'm all for an American duchess." His intense gaze held mine. His eyes sparkled. There was no sarcasm in his tone, only amusement and flirtation. "Guess I should have brought my classic Mustang." He glanced at Riggins. "Who are these beautiful women?"

"Lazer Grayson—Sid and Haley Hamilton. Ladies, Lazer." Riggins nodded between us.

Another footman arrived to park Lazer's car and take his luggage to his room. Riggins directed him to the Presidential Suite.

"Jus and Kay and Lady Rose are already here. Thorne will arrive later." Riggins put his hand in the small of my back, where I felt it acutely. "Come in and join the party. Once you've freshened up and settled in your rooms, we'll take a tour of the house and grounds." He gave me an intimate look. "That's the whole point of the weekend, isn't it?"

"Is it?" I held his gaze and raised an eyebrow. "That's what Lady Rose wanted, anyway." We all knew the whole point was something else entirely.

"Dinner is promptly at eight tonight. Our chef is an absolute tyrant. She won't tolerate any tardiness. In the spirit of the theme for the weekend, a gong will announce dinner." Riggins offered Sid and I each an arm and led us into the great hall of the castle. "That gives us a few hours for the tour before we have to dress for dinner."

The great hall, which doubled as the lobby in the modern era, was decorated ornately in the dark colors of the Victorian age. Deep brown solid wood floors and inset wood paneling on the walls. A fireplace with an intricately carved mantel and a roaring fire blazing. Rich, thick Persian carpets in dark red and cream. Greek statuary. Topiary trees. Doors to the dining room were closed.

The footman was waiting to take us to our rooms.

"See you back here in half an hour for the tour," Riggins said to us as he cast a quick look at Lazer.

Our suites were connected and shared a private Jacuzzi bath in the shape of a heart. A glass canister of rose petals sat on the edge of the bath, ripe for sprinkling in. The entire suite was lightly perfumed with lavender. My room was, obviously, deep pink, accented in gold. The bed was massive. Poppies adorned everything from the painting over the bed to the bedspread and rug.

The curtains were open, giving us a view of the English gardens. Sadly, this time of year wasn't their finest. The flowerbeds were covered in mulch. And although there were a few bushes with red winter berries of some kind, everything else was pretty stark. Sid and I had scoped it out online and seen pictures of the gardens in their summer glory. We'd have to come back in another season.

Sid's room was equally beautiful, with a gilded mirror and a heavy cherry wood armoire. All of the furniture was, of course, Victorian. Their website said much of it was original.

"I feel like we've stepped back in time," I said to Sid after the footman placed our suitcases on stands and departed. "Can you imagine Helen living here?"

Sid looked around. "I can almost feel her presence."

"You mean her mother's." I laughed, nervously. My pulse raced, but not with the pleasant sensation of being next to Riggins. Maybe it was fear. Or maybe it was the thrill of the hunt.

Sid fell into an armchair near the window in her room. "We're in deep crap, Hale." She waved her arm around, indicating the room. "This place definitely favors Lady Rose. Maybe we shouldn't have agreed—"

"We didn't have a choice," I reminded her. "Besides, we're on American ground. This place was built or, at least, reassembled by an American. We'll be fine."

I glanced at a clock on the dresser. "We'd better start getting ready for the tour. We want to stun everyone with the sheer volume of our wardrobe." I laughed as I got out my phone and scrolled through the pictures of the outfits the Flash girls had created for us. "Now what did Erica and Paige give us for a house tour? Looks like we have several options."

Sid nodded. "Hale?"

"Yeah?"

"Watch yourself around Lazer."

I frowned. "Why?"

"Riggins gave you a funny look when you talked to Lazer when he arrived. I think he's part of the test. The temptation. You were...a little too flirty with him."

I went cold. She was right. I'd known it immediately. I couldn't even deny it. I nodded. "You're right. I felt it, too." Then I grinned. "So how are we going to use Lazer to throw Lady Rose under the bus?"

Riggins

Thorne had been delayed waiting for the results of the DNA tests. Something was going on with them. Something he wouldn't say, but had him concerned. In the meantime, he was riding roughshod over the lab. And then he was meeting with an expert in DNA testing to go over the results with him.

Jus and I had talked when he and Kayla arrived. We were as stymied trying to find a way to counteract the Dead Duke's poison pill as we'd been the first day. I had the ring with me. Before the end of the weekend, I was going to have to propose to either Rose or Haley.

At this point, I was fifty-fifty, flipping and flopping on who I would choose. Each had their pros and cons. Haley was just too damned dangerous to my heart.

Lazer was the first of the guests to come down from his room and join me while we waited for the tour. "Your American choice, Haley, is cute. Her sister is a knockout. A little young, but wow."

"Stay away from Sid," I said, already sounding like a big brother. "Your job is to hit on Haley and Rose."

"Yeah, it's a tough job." Lazer paused. "Why does someone have to do it, Riggs? What's the rush to get a duchess and why is the press so up in arms and excited about it?"

"You haven't been following the story closely enough." I sighed. "Apparently I'm lonely, and since I'm the last of my family, I'm eager to find a duchess and produce an heir to protect my dukedom. I have a fear of dying early without a son to my name."

Lazer raised both eyebrows. "Seriously? I'll believe that when I see a flying pig. What's really going on?"

"Let's just say I'm under some pressure to marry."

"Someone has something on you." Lazer clicked his tongue. "I wouldn't have expected it of you, Riggins. I love intrigue. Who's blackmailing you into marrying? One of the girls?"

"Just charm the two candidates for duchess, will you?"

Jus and Kayla came down the stairs, interrupting our conversation, thankfully. Jus waved. "Lazer!"

The two men clapped each other on the back. Lazer hugged the very pregnant Kayla a little longer than was necessary, I thought. But Justin seemed fine with it.

"Look at you, glowing and beautiful," Lazer said to Kayla.

"Round and roly-poly, you mean." She smiled beautifully. "Aren't you going to tease me about swallowing a watermelon?"

"Who's eating watermelon? What have I missed?" Rose came down the stairs, elegantly dressed in wool slacks, a cashmere sweater, and diamonds.

She caught Lazer's attention immediately. It may have been my imagination, but the air fairly well crackled with sexual tension between them. She sized Lazer up, trying to mask her feelings, but failing. Not a good sign for me.

I was introducing her to Lazer when Sid and Haley came down. The contrast between the two women couldn't have been starker. Haley was dressed in boutique fashion from Flash—tight jeans, cotton blouse and sweater, canvas shoes, and costume jewelry. She looked young, fresh, and fashionable. My heart raced at the sight of her. Something about her...

Our tour guide arrived to take us around the house. "My name's Beth. I hope everyone's up for a tour of this exquisite house! I'm here to answer any questions as we go along."

"I feel like I'm in a scene from *Pride and Prejudice*," Haley said. "The one where Elizabeth takes a tour of Pemberley. What secrets will we find here at Wareswood?"

There was a big secret waiting for her in the dining room. I'd seen it when I toured the house before the guests arrived. I'd been unsettled by it. How would Haley react? I'd be watching her closely.

Haley

Our tour guide, Beth, was a middle-aged woman and assistant manager of the estate. She had a passion for the house that was infectious, and was equally enthusiastic and knowledgeable about what she laughingly called her charge. She began the tour in the great room, talking about the statues and how William Wares had purchased them at auction from an antiquities dealer in Greece shortly after the castle was built.

I was enthralled by the history and couldn't help picturing Helen and her older sister Clara, my great-grandma, whom I'd only just discovered when Mr. Thorne showed me my family tree, wandering through as girls, dressed in Victorian pinafores, playing in room after room with porcelain dolls and real china tea sets.

Their growing up had been miles away from my middle-class life. The money in my branch of the family tree hadn't made its way down to my generation. Clara had married beneath herself and fallen out of the wealthy class. Maybe even fallen out with the upper crust.

My mom had never talked much about her family. Before Mr. Thorne's arrival, I hadn't known I'd had a great-aunt who was a duchess. Only that there was some scandalous behavior way back in Mom's grandma's time. That her grandma had come from a wealthy household and made a marriage that the family believed was beneath her.

No mention of Helen, who'd married the financially savvy Dead Duke.

I hadn't been particularly interested in Helen or Clara before. Too many other things on my mind. With all that had been going on, I hadn't even bothered to research them.

Beth's stories of them piqued my interest and made them real. I had a family history that was actually pretty interesting.

"Helen, of course, became the Duchess of Witham when she came of age and married. She moved to England after her marriage and returned only occasionally for visits."

Sad. Had Helen felt that, too? Had she missed the city and country of her birth? Had it been lonely being an expat in England? Even though the climate was similar to ours, I loved Seattle and couldn't imagine leaving it for good. When I became duchess, *if* I became duchess, I would live at least half the year here. I made a mental note to make the stipulation part of the marriage contract.

On Thursday, I had visited the attorney Mr. Thorne had recommended. He was working on the paperwork and had requested the prenup Mr. Thorne was writing up as well. Just in case. Plan for all contingencies. Be prepared to act. But what were the contingencies? Did I have a decent shot?

When we were together, Riggins and I clicked. When we were apart, I couldn't get him out of my mind. I missed him. I could have spent every moment texting him. Wasn't that the test for love? Thinking of the other person when they were out of sight, but definitely not out of mind?

Hearing the history of Clara marrying beneath herself reminded me that from a social standpoint I was a bad catch. Well below his social class. Maybe marrying too far out of my class really would cause problems.

Rose was certainly more of his class than I was. And could teach him so much about the British upper class he was now a part of. I wondered if I should bow out. Just leave him to Rose. But my heart wouldn't let me. My gut feeling that she would be terrible for him kept me in the competition even though maybe it was just supremely biased.

As we toured the house, I was acutely aware of Riggins. I could feel his every move, even when he was out of my line of sight. I wished he could see how my heart ached for him. Or maybe that would only scare him away.

Rose was aristocratically bored. Been here, done this a thousand times. Wareswood Castle could hardly compare to the rich manor houses that she moved in as a matter of her birth. She didn't need a tour to see a house so much better than this, just an invitation to tea. The only thrill this house had for her was her connection to the late duchess who'd been a girl here. And so far, there hadn't been much about her in the tour.

Rose had a deep knowledge of artists and painters and fine old books that she didn't mind showing off. It would have been more annoying if she didn't carry herself with a certain grace and natural snobbiness that seemed to fit her social station. Yes, it was all too easy to picture her as the next duchess. And way too far of a stretch to see myself in the role.

What did I know about old paintings and how to preserve them? Or how to conduct household tours in a way that wasn't braggy, but fun and informative? Cultured.

Rose attached herself to Riggins, hanging on his arm and cooing in his ear when she wasn't coolly showing off.

I was relegated to the back of the pack. With Lazer paying particular attention to me, whispering jokes to me, and standing too close. At any other time this would have been a good thing. But right now I didn't need his rattling presence. Next to him I felt young, inexperienced, and uncultured.

Even still, it was hard *not* to be aware of Lazer Grayson. He was the hottest bachelor in Seattle, after all. And for good reason. Self-made billionaire. Smelled great. Looked better. Funny and charming. Flattering. He could put a bit of nerd on when he wanted. Knew how to flirt and did it shamelessly. He lacked only one quality in my opinion—he wasn't Riggins. But he was Riggins' spy, no doubt.

Chemistry and love were fickle creatures. Cupid pierced you with his arrow and made you blind to other candidates. I smiled at Lazer's jokes and made pleasant conversation. But I didn't flirt back. I'd been inoculated to his appeal by Riggins. Another type of girl might have tried to make Riggins jealous by flirting with Lazer. But that wasn't me.

My gaze kept following Riggins. I struggled to mask my jealousy. And fantasized about shoving Rose out of the way and taking her place. Instead, I distracted myself by listening to Beth and watching Justin and Kayla as they whispered to each other and gave each other admiring, loving looks. They were openly affectionate and so clearly belonged together. Kayla would reach up for no reason and stroke Justin's bearded cheek playfully. He kissed the top of her head. And patted her big belly proudly and protectively. They were completely adorable and so obviously in love.

Justin never let go of Kayla's hand. When the tour came to a stop, he hugged her from behind, putting his hand on her pregnant belly. Kayla smiled at him and ruffled his beard the wrong way until they both laughed.

That was the kind of relationship I wanted. With Riggins.

Sid connived and tried to help me out. Pushing us to Riggins' side, where we stood unnoticed while Rose monopolized him.

During the tour, I noticed Beth staring at me when she thought I wasn't looking. *Strange.* She took us through the sitting rooms, the study, walked past the kitchens with a quick explanation that they'd been totally renovated and modernized and weren't of much interest, the billiards room, the library, all the rooms on the main floor, pointing out paintings, artwork, and furniture and giving us each piece's history.

Finally, she ended the tour in the dining room. "You'll be dining here tonight and breakfasting here in the morning."

Beth stopped in front of a long, rectangular table. "Usually we have several large, round tables set up for guests. But for your stay we've moved in the original dining table. It can seat up to twenty if necessary." She began describing how it was acquired and telling us all about the manufacturer.

Rose was still hanging on Riggins' arm. "It's been brilliant seeing my biological family's ancestral home." She smiled at Riggins. "One can just picture Helen growing up here and having a lovely childhood. It's rather sad, though, that all the old houses are either open for tours or have been converted to something else. Your home, Witham House, is one of the few still privately held. No tours. It's an impressive accomplishment, given all the death taxes over the years and the increased labor costs."

She sighed, resigned. "Our house is open for tours four days a week April through September. It's a nuisance, really. But it pays the bills and keeps the paintings in the family. We have some fine ones, actually.

"I've been on our tour so many times that, frankly, I find it rather boring." She laughed softly. "You can only hear so much about the same old paintings and ancestors before you lose interest. It's nice to hear about new old paintings for once. New ones to me, anyway."

As if taking her cue from Lady Rose, Beth stopped in front of the largest wall of the dining room and pointed to the paintings overhead.

I'd been so preoccupied watching Rose and Riggins, I hadn't been paying much attention to what hung on the walls. During the tour I'd become kind of inured to all the fine art, and stopped really seeing much of it unless Beth called particular attention to a piece. I looked up, following where Beth pointed, and gasped. Hanging in the prime position over the fireplace was a picture of...me. Dressed as a Jazz Age high-fashion flapper, with long, loopy necklaces and all. The woman in the picture had bobbed silver hair, where my silver hair was long and in soft waves, but the resemblance was uncanny right down to the hair color.

Riggins was watching me closely. So was Beth. Suddenly I understood her interest in me and the odd looks she'd been giving me. As if they were in some kind of synchronized event, Justin, Kayla, Lazer, Sid, and Rose looked from the picture to me and back again. It was almost comical.

My mouth fell open. A prickle rose up my spine.

Beth held her hand up to the painting. "Helen, the Duchess of Witham. The painting was donated to Wareswood by the late duke." Beth laughed nervously and smiled at me. "I apologize for staring at you, Haley. You can certainly tell you're Helen's descendant. You look *just* like her. Or is it only me who sees the resemblance?"

The room had gone silent. Yeah, and now I knew why the Dead Duke was hellbent on me being the next duchess. I was a dead ringer for the woman hanging on the wall. Even down to the trendy silver color of my hair. Did Helen have that color naturally? Why hadn't I

ever thought to find a picture of her before? Why had-
n't my random Googling turned any up? What did the
Dead Duke look like in his youth? If Riggins was his
double, I was going to freak for real.

All eyes were on me, watching my reaction. My
mouth went dry. I swallowed hard and forced a smile as
I shrugged.

Rose looked nothing like Helen, and was obviously
pretending not to be unhappy about it. Which didn't
prove anything one way or the other. Why should a distant niece look like Helen? It was just creepy that I did.

Lazer took my arm. "There's no denying the late
duke had good taste."

Riggins flashed him a dagger look. That should have
been his line. But it wasn't. It had rolled off Lazer's
tongue, natural flattery.

Beth tried gamely to discuss the other paintings in
the room. But the crowd had lost interest and was giv-
en up to speculation and making up wild stories.

Beth finally had to give up. "That concludes the
tour. If anyone has any questions or would like to know
more, I'd be happy to help."

Kayla gasped suddenly and clutched her belly.

Justin took her by the arms and stared into her eyes
with the panicked look of an about-to-be-new-father.
"Kay?"

"Sorry!" Kayla laughed apologetically. "Particularly
strong baby kick. Your brothers are going to be
thrilled, Jus. This little girl kicks like a rugby player."
She gasped again.

"And she's tap-dancing on my bladder now. Sorry, everyone. I need to run. I think I'll go back to the room and get some rest before dinner." She sighed. "I haven't been this tired since the first few months. Carrying all this extra weight around."

Justin put his arm around her and offered to take her up.

"No, no. I'm fine." She kissed him quickly. "Stay here and visit with Riggins and Lazer."

Rose had been almost morbidly fascinated by Kayla's baby bump. She winced when Kayla misjudged the space she needed to squeeze around the table and caught it with her bump. Kayla didn't strike me as clumsy. She seemed generally graceful.

Rose had been trying to hide her reaction to Kayla's pregnancy. I sensed it made her uncomfortable and was an ugly distraction. Not something to look forward to. I hoped Riggins sensed it, too. I could evilly hope it was a deal breaker for him.

Riggins invited Lazer and Justin to play billiards.

"I'll walk up with you, Kayla," I offered.

Rose and Sid joined us. All of our rooms were in the same wing along the same hall. Kayla invited us in to see her room. "Each one's different. I love ours. You have to see it. You have to promise to let me see yours later."

She let us in. We wandered around looking at the various treasures, chatting while she used the bathroom.

"Worst things about being pregnant—having to use the bathroom every five minutes and being exhausted all the time. I'm sure you all noticed how many times I disappeared during the tour." She shook her head. "And I have a dark line up my stomach now. Worse—it's crooked."

"When are you due?" I asked her.

"Not soon enough!" She laughed again. "I'm due in March. You have to see the tub in there." She pointed to the bathroom. "It's big enough for two—baby and me. I'm looking forward to a nice soak later. Floating defies gravity and takes the weight off." She sighed. "Maybe I can get Jus to join me. We can hope the warm water lulls baby to sleep. She usually likes to keep me awake at night.

"And woe to us if we make love and wake her up. It's like making love with a basketball between us now, anyway. But when she starts kicking Jus!" She grinned. "Not very comfortable. Even hugging is awkward. All we can do is teepee hug. And even then the baby gets jealous and kicks Jus for sport."

Sid and I laughed. Rose was quiet. The pregnancy talk seemed to make her uncomfortable. She excused herself early, saying she was fighting a headache.

Sid and I went back to our room shortly after Rose left.

"How do you think it's going?" Sid asked when we were safely in our rooms.

I sighed. "Rose is waging an effective campaign. She seizes every opportunity to remind Riggins how aristocratic she is. How well she'd fit in in his new dukely world."

Sid pursed her mouth to the side. "Maybe. But since seeing that picture of Helen and how much you look like her, I'm willing to bet the Dead Duke will pull out all the stops to make sure you win this competition."

I laughed. "I wish that were true. I hate to tell you this, sis—but he's dead."

"That hasn't stopped him so far." Sid grinned.

iggins

  After defeating Justin and Lazer soundly in billiards, I headed to my room. Lazer claimed pool was more his game and challenged me to a video game marathon. He kept complaining—what kind of pool table didn't have pockets? A billiard table, buddy.

  I would have held his poor sportsmanship against him, but Lazer reported having as little success turning Haley's head as I'd had losing Rose. Which made me almost stupidly happy.

  Rose had nearly surgically attached herself to me all afternoon. I slid into my room, ready to grab my laptop and attend to a few business matters. As I closed the door, I froze.

What the hell? The lights were off. Candles were lit. And Rose was naked in my bed.

"Duke, what do you say we test our sexual chemistry before the wedding? I don't think I could accept a man who isn't a good lover?"

Hayley

Sid was tired, too, and wanted to rest before dinner. Which worried me, like always. I read in our room for a while, then decided to go out and explore the house again on my own. I wanted to see that painting of Helen again up close without anyone watching me. I couldn't get it out of my mind.

I shuddered to imagine how Rose would react with the picture of basically me hanging over us reminding her of my superior claim to the duchess title through a zillion courses at dinner. This wasn't what she'd bargained for when she'd wanted to see the castle. Then again, maybe it would fun watching her squirm.

Mr. Thorne would be arriving soon. I was half hoping to run into him and ask him about that painting. Though odds were he wouldn't know much about it. I slid silently out of my room so I wouldn't disturb Sid just as Riggins' door opened down the hall. My heart jumped into my throat. I started to smile and almost raised my hand to wave.

But it wasn't Riggins coming out of the room. Rose slid out with a sly look on her face. She looked my way. I went cold and numb. She caught my eye. I knew she did. Her sensual mouth molded into a smile. She looked away quickly, as if she was embarrassed. But she wanted me to see her. I knew she did. And to think the worst.

I kept walking, right through the great hall and into the cold, dark fog outside. I needed air. I needed to breathe.

Riggins

Thorne caught me as I stepped into the hall from my room, ready to head to the great hall to wait for my guests to come down to dinner. "Your Grace."

I invited him into my room so we could speak privately.

"Well? What's the news?" I crossed my arms, bracing myself.

"The DNA test results are surprising, sir. And confusing. Our expert is going over them again and preparing a report in layman's terms. I'd prefer to wait to deliver all the news until then. But I think you'll be pleased with the results. I certainly hope so."

Would I? I frowned. "I'm running out of time." Though I thought I knew my own mind now, I wanted to be sure of my choice. "When will the final report be ready?"

"Tomorrow morning at the latest, Your Grace. Maybe even later tonight."

"You'll let me know?"

"As soon as I have it, sir."

"Is Lady Rose still in the running?" I watched Thorne closely.

"I wouldn't rule her out just yet, sir." Thorne's smile was enigmatic.

He was holding something back from me. And seemed pleased about it.

Haley

I didn't know why I did it. I had a choice. I could have worn the red gown. Or the blue. Each equally gorgeous. But I chose the pink sequined evening gown for dinner. The color was nearly identical to the gown Helen was wearing in her picture above the dining table. The cut was similar, just an updated version. I couldn't say that I hadn't done it intentionally, even though I'd had no idea how I was going to choose between them. Until the last minute.

Sid tried to talk me out of it. "The comparison's too obvious."

"Is it?" I was hurt and hard inside. Riggins had told me no sex before marriage. I'd assumed that included Rose. And no, I couldn't know for certain. But she'd been in his room and come out looking smug and rumpled. Satisfied with herself and maybe just plain old satisfied, period.

"He needs to be reminded. I saw Rose coming out of his room, Sid. Remember?" My icy voice matched the way I felt inside. I didn't like either my voice or the feeling.

Sid winced. I'd told her all about it as soon as I returned to my room.

"It might not be what it looked like." Sid wasn't usually afraid to confront me, but this time she sounded timid and way too naïve.

"At the very least, it was exactly what Rose *wanted* it to look like. And that's enough." I held my chin high as I accessorized with a long strand of beads that could have stepped out of the 1920s as well.

"What's your plan?" Sid asked. "To bludgeon him with guilt?"

"Maybe."

Riggins was in the great hall, waiting at the bottom of the stairs talking to Mr. Thorne, Lazer, and Justin when Sid and I descended the stairs in our finery. Sid, of course, should have drawn all the attention.

My eyes met Riggins'. I kept my chin high and my back straight. His eyes went wide and dark. He paused midsentence. I'd made an impression. Good, damn him.

I was a shimmer of sequins and silk as Riggins offered me his arm. He leaned in and whispered in my ear, "You look hot."

"Thank you. And thanks to you for the Flash wardrobe. Erica and Paige are fashion geniuses. Be careful or someone will snatch them away from Flash and you."

He looked deep into my eyes. "Let them try. They'll never be able to match my counteroffer."

The gong sounded. A footman opened the doors to the dining room. "Dinner is served, Your Grace."

"Shall we?" Riggins said.

I smiled as seductively as I knew how. "Yes. I'm starved."

"Good." He led me into the dining room and pulled my chair out for me. He was seated at the head of the table with Mr. Thorne at the foot.

I was seated on one side of Riggins next to Justin with Sid next to him. Rose was on Riggins' other side between Lazer and Kayla at dinner.

"Isn't this jammy that we could all make it here this weekend?" Rose smiled at me, still smug. Still taunting.

I forced my insecurity aside.

"Wonderful." I returned her smile. Mine was as fake as hers was.

Her gaze flicked between me and the painting of Helen behind me. "Are you channeling Helen in the hopes of bringing out her mother's ghost?"

"Not at all. I purchased and packed this outfit without knowing about the painting. It's just coincidence. Like so many things here today." I kept smiling.

Riggins had planned a ten-course Victorian-style meal. I was a light eater by nature and small in size. Just a mouthful or two of each course and I was stuffed by the time the fifth one was served. Conversation flew. Witty banter. Teasing.

Riggins, Lazer, and Justin were old friends. They ribbed, teased, and generally tried to one-up each other in good fun. Thorne watched with quiet amusement, inserting his British humor at times.

Rose. She was classy and clearly skilled in social graces. But these were dire circumstances, and she obviously couldn't stand to be ignored or outdone. Her voice pitched a little too high. Her laugh became too shrill. She tried a little too hard to be the center of attention, or at least of Riggins' attention.

And Kayla seemed to make a point of pointing out the downsides of pregnancy just to see Rose's reaction. It was like she was goading her.

I suspected Kayla's pregnancy talk was Riggins' doing. Another of his tests. Like Lazer flirting with me and now with Rose.

What was Rose thinking? What were her battle and backup plans? Dangle another billionaire on a string? Keep him in reserve in case the billionaire duke didn't pan out? Was one billionaire as good as another? How could she resist the temptation of a second billionaire?

Riggins paid a great deal of attention to me. Even though I was upset with him, and had no right to be, I couldn't help flirting back and falling back into our comfortable roles.

"British for appetizer?" I said to him when the first course arrived.

"Entrée." His foot brushed mine beneath the table.

"You've been studying!" Despite the tension, I was enjoying myself.

It was almost midnight when the after-dinner coffee and drinks were finally cleared.

Kayla yawned. "I'm sorry, but I'm going to have to bail on you all and go to bed."

Justin held her chair for her. The men all stood.

"I'm going to turn in, too." Justin took his wife's hand.

I imagined they wanted to try out that bathtub.

"Watch out for ghosts." Riggins laughed. "Grace Wares is supposed to haunt the castle at night. Midnight is her favorite hour."

Kayla shook her head. "You're awful, Riggins, scaring everyone just before bed." She cupped her belly. "Don't listen to him, baby. Mama's here to protect you." She smiled at Riggins and gave him a hug.

To my surprise, she came over and hugged me, too. As she pulled me close, she whispered in my ear, "I hope you win. Don't let Rose get the best of you. And don't be afraid. Some of the greatest loves and best marriages started in unconventional circumstances. Take it from me."

After she and Justin left, Mr. Thorne said goodnight. Sid went up to bed.

Lazer took Rose's arm and asked her to go on a ghost hunt with him. "I have all the equipment." His tone was clearly lustful and full of innuendo.

Riggins offered to walk me up, and took my hand. "I didn't get a chance to ask you—what do you think of the painting of Helen?"

"You mean, what do I think about her looking like me?"

"She came first, so you must look like her." He smiled that lovely smile that made his eyes crinkle.

"Is that how it goes?" I shrugged. "It's eerie. But at least it explains why the Dead Duke wants me to be your duchess." I didn't see any harm in reminding him who the once and true duchess *should* be. "It's odd, though, how genetics work. People say I look more like my mom than my dad. But Mom didn't look like Helen, even though she was one generation closer to her."

He grinned. "Genetics are a mystery."

"I was wondering—do you look at all like the Dead Duke? Wouldn't that be the ultimate joke of fate?"

"We'll have to find out. Maybe Thorne has a picture of him."

"In his prime. Not as an old, wrinkly hundred-something-year-old. That won't be a fair comparison."

Riggins came to a stop in front of a room, but it wasn't mine.

"I'm there." I pointed to my room.

"I know." His eyes sparkled. "This is my room. It's the King's Suite. Supposedly King George V spent a night here once. Would you like to see it?"

My heart pounded in my ears as I nodded, unsure what, exactly, he was asking. "Sure."

He opened the door. A fire crackled in the fireplace. Electric candles sparkled on the nightstands. The four-poster bed was expertly turned down. Maid service had been in.

Before I could react, Riggins pulled me into his arms, cupped the back of my head, and tilted my face to his. "You look beautiful tonight, Haley. Absolutely stunning."

His lips came down on mine, gently at first. I opened my mouth to him as he pressed me against him, and wrapped my arms around his neck.

Kissing Riggins wiped all rational thought from my mind. He tasted good. He knew how to kiss. My heart sang. My heart raced. If he was just leading me on...

His kisses slid from my mouth to my chin. He lifted the hair from my neck and trailed hot, insistent kisses down it while I grasped his hair and held his head to me, heart pounding so loudly he had to have heard it.

He kissed the side of my neck, sucking, licking, teasing. I arched my neck back, encouraging him to kiss the hollow. Gasping as his kisses trailed down to the tops of my breasts.

"I've been wanting to do this all night," he murmured as he slid the straps of my gown off my shoulders. "I can't stop thinking about you, Haley."

He kissed my shoulders and the hollow where my pulse leaped for him. He shrugged out of his dinner jacket. "You're naked beneath this dress, aren't you? Your bouncing breasts have been making me hard all through dinner. You make me crazy with want."

I loosened his tie and slid it off. Unbuttoned his shirt and pulled it loose from his pants. *What are you doing, Haley? What are we doing? What does this mean?*

He swept his hands through my hair, pulled me close again, kissed the tops of my breasts, unzipped the back of my dress, and slid it off.

I *was* naked beneath that dress. Or nearly so. I wore only a sheer thong panty and my heels. The firelight flickered over my bare skin and lit the angles of Riggins' face. He scooped me into his arms and carried me to the bed, laying me softly down on my back. Staring at me, he took his shirt and undershirt off. Revealing a hot body beneath. Sculpted abs. Firm biceps. A hard chest that rippled as he kicked off his shoes.

He was definitely eye candy. But that wasn't what I liked best about him. Not that or his money. I just liked him—his wit, the way he smiled, the whole package.

When he stared at them, my breasts budded up in the heat of the fire. I was terrified. But my fear didn't keep me from wanting him. *So* badly. Enough to face my fears and expose the inexperience I'd kept from everyone. But I wanted him to want me for more than just a night. I didn't want to our first time together to be an experiment. Or a test.

I wanted it to mean something to him. I'd given him the wrong impression by coming into his room. I hadn't meant—

Before I could say any of that, he lay down next to me on the bed, slid a finger beneath my thong, and bent to gently suck my breast.

I whispered his name as his finger pleasured me and his hot mouth took possession of my breasts. He had me just where he wanted me. "Riggins. *Riggins.*"

His finger slid inside me. Then another. He knew exactly what he was doing as he found and caressed my clit. He was so experienced, and I...

Was on the edge of pleasure. With a secret. "This isn't fair. I'm naked and you're still half dressed."

"I'm okay with that. For now." His voice was deep and sexy. His eyes dark. "I'm enjoying looking at you. Soon enough I'll get naked, too."

I thought my heart was going to hammer out of my chest. "Riggins, I don't want this to be a test..."

"It's not a test." His thumb caressed me. "I *want* you." He circled my nipple with his tongue.

I was getting nearer and nearer the edge, trying to hold back. Wondering what I should do. "I thought you said we wouldn't..."

I didn't want to tell him. I didn't want to say it. But...

"Riggins, I'm a virgin."

He pulled away from my breast and stroked my hair, smiling at me, his face shadowed by the fire behind him. "Yeah? Just now, I pretty much guessed."

I blushed.

He hadn't removed his fingers. He covered my mouth with his, silencing my protests, thrusting his fingers deep inside of me until I lost myself in the pleasure.

"Let yourself go, Haley," he whispered, and sucked my breast until I gasped.

I hadn't thought I'd needed or wanted his permission. But now that I had it, I relaxed, losing myself in him. I climaxed with my head thrown back, my eyes closed, and his name on my lips.

"Haley—"

A scream pierced the silence. Then another. A high-pitched female voice that sounded almost inhuman shrieked in the hall.

Riggins swore beneath his breath, released me, grabbed his shirt, and ran into the hall. I slid into my dress and shoes, zipping myself up as I raced to the door.

"I saw her! I saw the ghost. I saw Grace." Lady Rose was pale and white.

Was she really that good an actress? I shivered, feeling the hair stand up on the back of my neck.

Lazer came racing around the corner. "Where? How did I miss her?"

"There. She was there!" Rose pointed to the end of the hall and the window.

Outside, the fog had rolled in. When her gaze met mine, she was both smug and angry. She knew what she'd interrupted. She'd done it intentionally.

Thorne came out of his room. Kayla and Justin poked their heads out of theirs. Sid came out into the hall in her robe, carrying a vase, ready to clobber any ethereal beings with the strictly material world. I hoped the vase she'd chosen wasn't an expensive antique. But, unlike the rest of us, at least she'd come prepared with *something*.

Lazer came up behind her, carrying some kind of camera and electronic gear. "EVP recorder and full-spectrum camera. This would work better, in this case, I think."

Justin shook his head. "Since when have you had ghost-hunting equipment?"

Lazer grinned. "Since I bought it for the weekend." He pushed the playback button. "Damn. All I got was Rose's scream."

"Sorry." Now that she'd gotten what she wanted, Rose put on a pretty pout and tried to look a little contrite. "I simply saw her and didn't think." She put her arms around herself.

Lazer wrapped his suit coat around her shoulders. I resisted rolling my eyes. Obvious bitch.

"Nothing to see here now." Riggins shook his head. "Show's over."

"Everyone back to your *own* rooms." Justin put his arm around Kayla. "Is that what you're saying, Riggs? What a house party!"

Riggins turned to me. "I'll walk you to your room."

People, meaning Rose among them, were still lingering in the hall, so he could hardly kiss me goodnight. "See you in the morning." He kissed my cheek. "Goodnight."

"She did that on purpose," Sid said when we were both safely locked in for the night and the door barred against all specters. "Rose couldn't stand the thought of you having Riggins to yourself."

I was embarrassed. Maybe I'd just blown it forever with Riggins now that he knew my secret. Not even Sid knew. I might have let her have an accidental impression of how far I'd gone with some of the guys I'd dated. If Riggins wanted an experienced woman, I wasn't it.

"How was it?" Sid asked. "What did he say? Did he propose?"

I shook my head.

"Do you think he will?"

"I have no idea."

CHAPTER ELEVEN

iggins

$\mathcal{R}$ I woke early. I'd made up my mind. I knew who the next duchess would be.

I showered. Shaved. Dressed carefully. Rehearsed the words I planned to say when the time came. My phone was on the nightstand with my wallet. I was about to stuff it in my pocket when I got a text from Thorne.

The DNA expert's report is in. Let's meet later to discuss particulars and implications.

He linked to a website with a detailed report. I took a minute to review the results. Now there were no obstacles. And no escape from marriage.

I grabbed the antique velvet ring box with Helen's engagement ring inside and took a deep breath. I'd propose before breakfast so we could announce it to our friends and sell this relationship. I'd worry about the details later.

The castle was quiet. Just the sounds of the staff downstairs. The hall was empty. This wasn't the way I'd planned my life. But now I knew which woman I would share it with. At least for a while.

I strode down the hall and paused before her door. Another deep breath. I knocked, ready to get down on one knee if necessary, clutching the ring box in my pocket.

I heard footsteps on the other side of the door. My heart raced, though why I should have been nervous I didn't know.

The door swung open.

"Rose?"

Gina Robinson is the award-winning author of the romantic comedy Switched at Marriage serial, contemporary new adult romances *Rushed, Crushed, Hushed, Reckless Longing, Reckless Secrets,* and *Reckless Together* and the Agent Ex series of humorous romantic suspense novels. She's currently working on the next Jet City Billionaire romance.

Connect with Gina Online:

My Website: http://www.ginarobinson.com/
Twitter: @ginamrobinson
Facebook: www.facebook.com/GinaRobinsonAuthor

www.ingramcontent.com/pod-product-compliance
Lightning Source LLC
Chambersburg PA
CBHW070926130626
46555CB00001B/301